New Dawn
on
Rocky Ridge

Roger Lea MacBride

Illustrated by Dan Andreasen

HarperTrophy®
A Division of HarperCollins*Publishers*

*To Jean Coday, who manages not only
to do many things, but to do them well;
Laura would recognize her in a minute.*

Little House®, 🎬®, Harper Trophy®, and The Rose Years™
are trademarks of HarperCollins Publishers Inc.

New Dawn on Rocky Ridge
Text copyright © 1997 Little House Heritage Trust
Illustrations copyright © 1997 by Dan Andreasen

Library of Congress Cataloging-in-Publication Data
MacBride, Roger Lea, 1929–1995.
    New dawn on Rocky Ridge / Roger Lea MacBride ; illustrated by Dan
Andreasen.
        p.   cm.
    Summary: While living on Rocky Ridge Farm in Missouri, thirteen-
year-old Rose celebrates the turn of the twentieth century and begins to
wonder about her future.
    ISBN 0-06-024971-4. — ISBN 0-06-440581-8 (pbk.)
    1. Wilder, Laura Ingalls, 1867–1957—Juvenile fiction.   [1. Wilder, Laura
Ingalls, 1867–1957—Fiction.   2. Frontier and pioneer life—Missouri—
Fiction.   3. Missouri—Fiction.]   I. Andreasen, Dan, ill.   II. Title.
PZ7.M12255Nj   1997   97-4990
[Fic]—dc21   CIP
                                                                                                    AC

Typography by Alicia Mikles
First Harper Trophy edition, 1997
❖
Visit us on the World Wide Web!
www.littlehousebooks.com

Dear Reader:

The book you hold in your hands is the work of my father, Roger Lea MacBride. It continues the childhood story of Rose Wilder Lane, and her mother and father, Laura Ingalls and Almanzo Wilder. Rose treated my father much as she would have treated a grandson and told him many stories about what it was like growing up in Missouri almost a hundred years ago. Dad took those stories and spun them into a series of books based on the facts of Rose's life. New Dawn on Rocky Ridge is the sixth of those books.

I'm sorry to have to tell you that my father has passed away. But my sadness is softened some because his work, the stories of Rose's early life, will continue. He left four partially completed manuscripts that continue Rose's tale, right up to the time she is seventeen years old and ready to leave home to start a life of her own.

There will be two more books after this. With the help of the editors at HarperCollins, we will be able to complete the story of Rose and her family as they come into the modern age of the telephone and automobile.

I am very pleased that these stories will be available to new generations of readers. You will find, as I did, that in a hundred years the things young people think and worry about haven't changed all that much.

Abigail MacBride Allen

Contents

Century's End

The mild, drizzly weather that had followed Christmas finally broke, and the last day of the old century dawned clear and biting cold. The frosty air stung Rose's nostrils, and the wind made her eyes water. But the bright sun warmed her cheeks and lay like a cozy shawl on the shoulders of her chore dress.

From the kitchen door she looked out onto the backyard. She didn't see the frozen mud scarred by wagon tracks and hoof marks. She didn't see the railroad grade blackened with coal soot. She didn't even see the wash on the line, waiting to be labored over with the heavy irons, and then neatly folded.

Instead she saw the sunlight glinting off the icy puddles. She heard the telegraph wires singing in the wind. Gusts whipped the sheets she had hung out to bleach that morning. They shimmered as white and fresh as a hillside of apple blossoms and snapped cheerfully, like proud flags on Independence Day.

The strong light made ordinary things look sharp and solid, as if seen through a stereoscope. On this day, at century's end, Rose's eyes looked at her everyday world as if they were seeing it for the first time.

"For goodness sake, Rose," Mama's voice called out from behind her in the warm kitchen. "Please shut that door before we all catch our death of cold."

Rose pulled the door closed behind her, filled her lungs, and crossed the backyard with the water bucket swinging from her hand. The cold air flowed like water around her bare legs, but she felt a fire glowing within that no cold could reach. This was New

Year's Eve, the start of the twentieth century. Just thinking of it sent a thrill along all her nerves.

"Happy New Year!" she cried out to Mama's Leghorn chickens. The snowy hens were too busy pecking at the frozen earth to pay her any mind. Bunting, the Jersey milk cow, lifted her head from her trough in the barn lot and lowed a single half-questioning note. Then she stuck her wet nose back into the trough and bit another mouthful of hay.

Rose pumped the squeaky handle until the water came. She watched a lonely castle of clouds hurry past overhead. The bowl of pure blue sky glowed with light. Suddenly the cloud let down a snow shower. Flakes as fine as dust blew about the barn lot, dancing in the silvery light like confetti and powdering the roofs like cake sugar.

"January the first, nineteen hundred and aught," Rose said aloud. Never before had anyone lived in a year that began with nineteen hundred. Of course, every year was new. But this was something special, the changing of the centuries. In a person's whole lifetime, that could happen only once.

Everyone in town had been talking about it for months. In Rose's Fifth Reader class her new teacher, Professor Bland, taught the history of the century—from the inventions of the steamboat and cotton gin to the telephone and motor car; from the expedition of Lewis and Clark, through the Civil War, right up to the war with Spain that had happened just two years ago.

"In one hundred short years, America has grown from a savage wilderness to the greatest, richest nation on earth," Professor Bland told the scholars. "You must study the past to prepare yourselves to inherit the future."

The tattered newspapers and magazines that Papa brought home from the railroad depot, left behind in the waiting room by traveling men, brimmed with stories about the condition of the country and the world. Rose especially liked to read articles forecasting the future. Each issue had stories predicting everything from flying machines to the most outlandish fashions.

There was so much to look forward to. New inventions were making life easier, taking the drudgery out of housework, and the country was in a boom. But some people weren't happy.

Rose read that in San Francisco people complained that Chinese immigrants were taking away the jobs of hard-working fathers. The newspapers said the Chinese worked for little money and didn't want to become good Americans.

Rose had never met anyone from China. But she knew it was no sin to be poor. And after all, it was poor immigrants who had settled America and built it up—poor immigrants from all over the world.

In the East, people complained about immigrants from Europe. In a single day in New York City, where the Statue of Liberty watched over the harbor, ships brought ten thousand poor immigrants yearning for freedom. That was twenty times the number of people who lived in Mansfield, the little town in the Ozarks where Rose lived. In one day! So many foreigners were coming that in time there would hardly be any Americans left in America.

Rose knew, of course, that there really were no Americans, except the Indians who were here first. Everyone else was an immigrant, or came from immigrant ancestors. Rose's family had come from Europe, as long as one hundred and seventy years before. But now the country was bulging with immigrants, and how would they all live?

The cities were crowding up, because Americans were going there, too, leaving the old folks to keep up the farms. And everywhere the Negroes suffered almost the same as when they had been slaves. There had been horrible riots in New York City when some white people threw paving stones at Negroes.

In the South, in the dark of night, white men dragged Negro men out of their beds and hanged them without any justice. That was called lynching, and there had been a hundred lynchings in a single year.

Rose and Mama and Papa often read the papers together at night at the dining-room table. Mama put out a bowl of apples, and they huddled around the circle of light from the kerosene lamp, talking about the stories they read.

"Why are people so cruel to each other?" Rose wondered.

"I don't quite know," Mama said sorrowfully, reaching out to turn up the wick a little. "I suppose it's a question of money. 'A poor man is hated even by his own neighbors, but the rich man has many friends.'"

Papa drew on his pipe. "Seems as if the country's going great guns and, all at the same time, headed for wrack and ruin." The room filled with the woodsy scent of tobacco smoke. "I'd say we're in a good safe place right here. But I don't much like the future I see out there, way things are going."

Some of those predictions were truly frightening. A famous prognosticator said the earth would heave up at midnight, at the dawn of the new century. There would be a terrible cataclysm along the Mississippi River. The land would open up and swallow whole towns. The ground would quiver until the soil turned to mud. Nothing and no one would be left, and the earth would keep shaking for a long time after.

That was something to think about in the Ozark Mountains of Missouri, where Rose lived with Mama and Papa. There had been a terrible earthquake in Missouri a long time before, in 1811. The New Madrid earthquake had swallowed whole towns and changed the course of the river. People had felt the earth's rumbling as far away as Washington, D.C.

Some said it was the wrath of God that did it, and He would visit His wrath again for all the sins of mankind. The newspaper articles said some people so believed this was true that they had given away all their money and possessions, to be better prepared for the Judgment Day. They called those people Earthquake Christians.

"It just proves there's no need to sow foolishness," Mama said, testing the heat of the oven with her hand. "It grows like weeds all of its own."

Rose chuckled as she turned the page of the *Chicago Interocean* and smoothed it flat on the kitchen table. Mama had a colorful saying for everything.

Mama shut the oven door on a sweet potato pie they would take to the New Year's Eve watch party at church that night. The kitchen filled with its nutty sweet fragrance.

"Still, I think it would be wonderfully interesting to see an earthquake," Rose mused, turning another page. "I mean, after it was finished. If no one could be hurt. Do you really think there won't be one?"

"There's always some rascal drumming up nonsense to panic folks," said Mama, wiping her hands on her apron and peering over Rose's shoulder. "Look," she said. "There's a picture of a Fido dog."

At the sound of his name, Fido raised his head from where he lay warming himself by the stove. He looked at Rose and Mama with bright eyes, his little head cocked and black ears perked. Then he lay down again with a sigh.

Together Mama and Rose looked at an advertisement for the Victor Talking Machine. There was a picture of the machine. It was a wooden box with a crank. Sticking out was a metal horn that looked like the tin trumpets older folks held to their ears to hear better, except sound was supposed to come out of it instead of going in.

A little white dog with black ears that looked like Fido sat in front of the machine, his head cocked. He was listening to "His Master's Voice" coming from the trumpet.

Another picture showed a ballroom full of dancing couples. The women had piled their thick hair into luxurious pompadours and wore low-cut ball gowns that left their backs and shoulders shockingly bare.

"My land, look at those dresses," Mama said, adding a clucking sound. "If any woman in this town dared step out her door in one, she'd be the scandal of all of Wright County."

But Rose thought those women looked impossibly elegant with their long embroidered hems sweeping the floor. The men stood sleek and tall in their black jackets with tails, and crisp boiled collars with white bow ties. Their faces were clean-shaven, the new style that hadn't yet come to Mansfield. Every grown-up man Rose had ever known wore a mustache, like Papa, or a full beard. Rose decided she liked the new style better. Beards made men look all the same, especially with their hats on.

The couples in the advertisement picture stepped and twirled to music from the talking machine. "Loud enough for dancing," bragged the advertisement.

"How can it work?" Rose wondered. "I can't think how they could make sound come out of a flat old plate."

"Neither can I," said Mama. She untied her apron and hung it on its hook by the backdoor. "I can't think the sound of it would ever be as good as a living fiddler or singer. But at the rate machines are taking up the work of humans, I wouldn't wonder if one day we won't have to lift a finger even to eat.

"Life is getting to be so complicated, and costly," she went on, sitting down with a cup of tea. "And it seems folks are in such a hurry to get ahead, they are throwing civility out of the window. I shouldn't like to see where all this change is taking the world."

Rose wished Mama and Papa wouldn't speak so. The future had become terribly important to her. She had just turned thirteen some weeks before. She was becoming a young lady and thinking more and more as a person with choices to make.

She had begun to wonder about her future in a way she never had before. She could see now that in just a few more years she would have her own life, apart from Mama and Papa. She wanted to know what that life might be like, so she read those predictions with a hungry and hopeful eye.

I Could Do It

After the morning church service, Rose walked home with Mama, Papa, and the Cooleys. Mama and Mrs. Cooley chatted about plans for the watch party and gossiped about Reverend Mays.

Mrs. Cooley was Mama's oldest and dearest friend, from the time the two families had lived in South Dakota, before they emigrated in wagons together to Missouri. Mr. Cooley had been Papa's best friend, but he was killed in a train wreck two years before.

Paul and George were Mrs. Cooley's sons and Rose's oldest friends, from the time Rose first started to school. Paul would be sixteen soon, nearly a man in Rose's eyes. George was almost a year older than Rose. He would be fourteen in the new year.

Paul was the most handsome boy in school, even in the whole town, Rose thought. He was her best friend, like a big brother, and something more, too. But she kept that extra feeling to herself. The only person she ever told was Blanche Coday, her girlfriend from school.

Rose was too young to have a beau. But when she did, the only boy she could ever imagine going buggy-riding with on Sundays would be Paul.

"I wonder if we shouldn't have a pie supper in January for Reverend Mays and his family," Mama said, hugging herself against a blast of frigid air. The dark-blue feather sticking out of her hat fluttered in the breeze. The rhythmic smack of hammers echoed from the depot, across the town square. Carpenters were getting ready for the fireworks that night, and putting up a big pole for a barrel fire.

"Mrs. Deaver was telling me that Mrs. Mays lost most of her garden in that terrible hailstorm last August. I reckon she'll have a hard way to go this winter, with eight young mouths to fill."

"Yes," Mrs. Cooley said brightly, hitching up the hem of her skirt as she stepped off the sidewalk to cross the street. "I had heard that as well. I don't see how folks can manage with such a large family these days, and the cost of everything gone up so. A pie supper would break up the winter some, too. It would be pleasant to have an extra entertainment."

Reverend Mays and his family were very popular with the congregation, and everyone was fiercely proud of the brand-new Methodist Church they had built only that fall. Reverend Mays had led the very first service in it just a week earlier, on Christmas Eve. The Mays family was poor. Everyone wanted to help them, and especially to keep Reverend Mays in Mansfield.

The Wilders and Cooleys had gone to Prairie Hollow Church since they first moved to the Ozark Mountains from South Dakota five years before. It was the only one in town. There were small log churches out in the country, hidden in shady hollows at the end of faint wagon tracks. But only farm families belonged to them, and folks in town wouldn't ever go to one. Mama said the preachers shouted their sermons, and the services could be very rowdy.

The best families in Mansfield—the bankers and storekeepers—had built Prairie Hollow Church when the town was new, sixteen years ago. They all went there. The women and young ladies of those families wore the finest dresses money could buy. The men drove beautiful buggies with brass-trimmed harness. And Reverend Davis gave long, sober sermons about hard work and temperance.

Mama had wished for a church where she needn't feel shy about wearing her same best dress two Sundays in a row. Her wish came true that summer when one of the owners of the railroad, Mr. F. M. Mansfield, made a gift of the land to build it on. The town was named after Mr. Mansfield, because he had owned the land before the railroad came through and the depot was built.

Mama, Papa, Mrs. Cooley, and many other people in town met and founded a Methodist congregation, and hired Reverend Mays for their first minister. He had been a traveling preacher before that. Now he could stay close to his family. Mr. Reynolds let them hold their services in an empty room over his store while they built the new church.

Papa drove loads of lumber and other supplies with his draywagon. Paul and George helped the carpenters and painters. Rose and Mama and Mrs. Cooley kept the men fed, and sewed curtains for the beautiful arched windows.

The new church was so much cozier than Prairie Hollow, which had a high vaulted ceiling and stood on a bare rise just south of the railroad tracks. The Methodist Church was on the quiet north side of town, on the Hartville Road. Three oak trees around it would shade it from the summer sun.

The church had two small wings, with a graceful peaked bell tower in between. Because the ceilings were lower than in Prairie Hollow, the heater stoves kept the church warmer on cold Sunday mornings. Rose loved the clean scent of new wood and fresh paint, and Reverend Mays gave the most entertaining sermons, full of stories told in plain language. Even she liked going to church now.

Rose, Paul, and George dawdled in the street at the corner by the livery stable waiting for Mama, Papa, and Mrs. Cooley to catch up. The grown-ups strolled so slowly on Sundays, like cows grazing a pasture. They had stopped to chat with Mrs. Gaskill, a neighbor of Rose's family who was taking some of her eggs to her sister's house to make an eggnog. Papa tipped his hat, keeping one hand on Mama's arm. Mrs. Cooley's hands fluttered as she talked.

Paul stamped his feet impatiently and made rings of steam with his breath. Rose clapped her mittens over her ears trying to warm them up.

"I hope Reverend Mays doesn't keep us stuck in our seats all night," Paul said. His cheeks flared pink with cold, and he kept his hands jammed into his coat pockets. "I'd hate like anything to miss the fireworks and all. Jessie Gaskill says Reverend Davis won't let the Prairie Hollow congregation go 'til midnight's come and gone. He's such an old stick-in-the-mud."

"Reverend Mays wouldn't dare," said Rose, watching two men on ladders hang red, white, and blue bunting over Reynolds' Store. The wind tore the banner from the hands of one of them, and he let out an angry shout. "Would he?" she said.

"I don't care if he does," George declared. A team of horses pulling a fancy buggy with red wheels came tearing around the corner. George jumped out of the way just in time. The driver was a man in a dark duster. He clenched a cigar in his teeth and drove with both hands tight on the reins. He stared straight ahead as the team and rig thundered past, throwing up bits of frozen mud and manure.

"Hey, where's the fire, Mr. Fancy Pants!" George shouted, shaking his fist. The buggy careened around the next corner and disappeared. "I'm not sittin' in no church when every boy in town's going to be in the square. No sirree!"

"You'll sit where you're told, as long as I say," plump Mrs. Cooley chided from the sidewalk. "And mind your mouth, young man. Howling in the street at strangers is not my notion of good manners."

"But Mama, he near ran me . . ."

"Shut up, George," Paul growled.

George grumbled once and fell silent.

The two families said their good-byes and headed their separate ways home. Those two boys couldn't be more different if they had been born to different families, Rose thought.

Mr. Cooley had been a strict father. Neither of them had dared make him cross, not if they could help it. He believed sparing the rod spoiled the child. Both boys had tried hard to please him. Paul was the more agreeable and dependable. When he was just ten years old, he drove a covered wagon and a team of big horses all the way from South Dakota to Missouri. George always was a bit troublesome, and Rose often found his boyish antics annoying.

After Mr. Cooley died, both boys became more of what they were. George grew especially bumptious, getting into mischief at school, teasing the girls, scrapping with other boys.

Paul had grown more sober and thoughtful. He was older now and did a man's work, handling baggage at the depot to earn money to help his mother with the house expenses. But he still kept up with his school studies. He even had a dream for his future.

Sometimes Rose would stop at the Cooleys' small house on the north side of town to visit for a few minutes on her way to or from an errand. Mrs. Cooley was a little round-faced woman with a brisk, bustling manner. She always stood at the door to see that the boys wiped their feet before they went in. Her house was very neat. The ingrain carpet on the front-room floor was swept until every thread showed. The center table had a crocheted tidy on it and a Bible and a polished seashell.

"Come in and look what I've got in the shed," Paul had said one day. Rose followed him around to the back of the house. He had cleared out the woodshed and put in a table and a chair. On the table stood a telegraphic sounder and key, and a round, red, dry battery. Mr. Nickles, the stationmaster, had given him an old set.

"I'm going to learn to be an operator," he said earnestly, brushing a lock of his wavy black hair off his forehead. "I've got most of the alphabet already. Listen."

He put his finger on the key, pressed it, and made the instrument click, just the way the operator did at the depot.

"I'm practicing receiving, listening to the

wires in the depot. Telegraph operators make as much as seventy dollars a month, and some of them, on the fast wires, make a hundred. I guess the train dispatcher makes more than that. Look at Thomas Edison. He started as a telegraph operator."

He let Rose press the key a few times. "I could do it. I know I could," she said. Seventy dollars a month! In a whole year Mama couldn't make as much from her egg money.

"I reckon you could," he said. "After all, you're the best scholar in the whole school. But that's a fella's sort of work. There's plenty of rough types around a depot. Besides, a woman's place is in the home."

Rose clicked the key again. "A girl can do lots of things besides housework," she said, trying not to sound quarrelsome. "My aunt Eliza Jane worked as a government girl once, in Washington, D.C. Lots of women are teachers. Mama was a teacher once."

"Sure, Rose," Paul said, disconnecting the wires from the battery so it wouldn't run down. "But somebody's got to stay home and take care of the housekeeping. It's always been that way. Always will be."

Rose didn't see why that had to be true, but she kept her thoughts to herself. Paul was so earnest and determined about things. She just knew he really would be a telegraph operator one day, sending and decoding urgent messages, and getting the news before anyone else.

Paul wasn't like any of the other boys she knew. Most of them lived for mischief or lounged around the livery stable pitching horseshoes, sniggering at the rough language of the men, and drinking water from Mr. Hoover's bucket without so much as a thank-you.

Paul was kind and strong. He kept himself too busy with work and school and chores for any such foolishness. For two years now he had been like a father, taking care of his mother and watching out for George.

Rose thought no boy could be as good, and she couldn't help wondering if he would still like her when she was finally old enough to have a beau.

New Year's Eve

That was the noisiest Sunday anyone could remember. After dinner and all afternoon, the little town crackled with gunshots and firecrackers. At both churches the bells pealed on each hour, counting down the last moments of the old century. The passing trains blasted their shrill horns as they rumbled along the railroad grade that ran behind the house.

Along the frozen street in front of the house, boys rolled old barrels toward the square for the barrel fire. The air rang with their shouting and laughing. Wagons rattled past, almost as many as on Saturday, bringing farm families who would stay to watch the New Year in at the square.

Blanche Coday stopped by to invite Rose for a walk.

"Everyone is out and about," Blanche burbled happily. Her nose shone bright red, and she had tucked her curly black hair up into a hat made of sleek beaver fur. Her hands disappeared into a matching muff. She looked as pretty as the girls Rose saw in advertisements for skin cream.

"I never saw such a Sunday," Blanche went on. "All the boys have firecrackers and they don't care who they frighten with them. That wicked brother of mine, Walter, put some in the cookstove and scared poor Edwinna so. She dropped one of Mother's best platters. Smashed it to pieces! Can't you come out, just for a little while?"

"I can't," said Rose regretfully. Behind her back she clutched her dustrag. "I have to help Mama with the oyster stew and the baking and the housework. We're having company to supper."

Blanche's father owned Coday's Drugs. The Codays lived in one of the finest houses in town, and Blanche's mother kept a hired girl, Edwinna. Mama wouldn't have a hired girl, even if she could pay for one. She didn't like to have another woman underfoot.

Rose helped Mama bake four loaves of bread that afternoon, then a batch of sugar cookies. Finally they made a gingerbread to take to the Opera House, where the ladies from the Eastern Star would serve coffee, lemonade, and sweets. Rose finished dusting and then swept the parlor, the dining room, and the kitchen. They didn't have boarders just then, so at least she didn't have the added work of cleaning the two extra bedrooms.

She filled the woodbox, brought water to heat in the stove reservoir, and then ironed a fresh collar for Papa. Then she ironed Mama's shirtwaist, and the company tablecloth.

Rose worked as hard as any hired girl, maybe even harder, she grumbled to herself as she pressed at a stubborn wrinkle. More and more, as she had gotten older, she felt enslaved to the dishpan and the iron, the broom and the water bucket. Outside, on the streets of town, on the racing trains, all around the world, life passed her by. She was learning what grown women meant when they sighed wearily and said to each other, "A man's work lasts 'til set of sun, but woman's work is never done."

Rose hoped the future, with all the wonderful new conveniences it promised, would change that.

Her mood lifted when the table had finally been set and she could stand back for a moment to admire it. Rose had washed the chimneys of the two oil lamps until they gleamed. Their flames shone through the glass like bright stars. The warm light ran along the rims of the blue willowware plates, twinkled off the silverware, and reflected in the gold-leafed glass of the clock. Cedar boughs from Christmas still draped the windows, and Mama had put on the table a yellow china bowl with fresh twigs of orange-berried bittersweet.

That was a moment when Rose could appreciate the work it took to keep a tidy house, when it could be shared with friends and loved ones.

They were sharing their New Year's Eve supper with the Cooleys and the Bairds, who lived on the Wilders' farm, just a mile east of town. Abe Baird had been Papa's hired hand when Rose's family lived on Rocky Ridge Farm. That was the place Mama and Papa bought when they first moved to Missouri.

Abe and his little brother, Nate, had been living in a sharecropper's house nearby, on a farm owned by another family. Abe was a young man, and Nate was a year younger than Rose. When the family that owned the farm moved away, Papa bought the land and hired Abe to help him improve it, tend the crops, and cut timber. Abe and Nate Baird became like family to the Wilders.

Abe was a hard worker, and a wonderful storyteller and fiddler. Nate had been a scrappy little boy at first, but in time Rose and Mama had managed to tame him. Now he was a good student in school, and a friend to Rose. They especially shared a love for books, although Nate liked boys' adventure stories like *Ragged Dick* and Rose liked to read grown-up novels and history.

Abe had met and started sparking with Effie Stubbins, the daughter of another neighbor of the Wilders. They married, and Abe and Effie had twins, a little boy and a little girl. James and Elza were almost three years old.

The children were running about with confidence now, and James talked up a storm. He couldn't make his "r"s come out right, so he called Rose "Wose," which always made her giggle with delight. She loved them both dearly, but to herself she admitted that she liked James a little bit better. Elza was shy, and Rose could hardly tell what the little girl was thinking.

After the spring when the twins were born, a long drought stunted the crops. Then a fire burned over some of their fields. That fall Mama and Papa decided it would be better to live in town. They moved out of the farm into a house that Grandfather Wilder had bought for Papa from Mrs. Cooley.

The Bairds moved into the little house on Rocky Ridge Farm, and they gave Mama and Papa a share of the crops and timber money for their rent. That way the farm could be kept up, and the Wilders would have food to last the winter. The house in town had space for only a small garden.

Inside it was much larger than the farm house. For the first time Mama had a real parlor. Papa had bought her a set of parlor furniture with a tête-à-tête, a rocker, an easy chair, and an armless parlor chair. Every piece was covered in a beautiful bottle-green tapestry with yellow and pink flowers all over.

The house had two extra bedrooms that they let out to boarders to make extra cash money. And sometimes other men came and paid Mama to eat her cooking, instead of taking their meals in the hotel or the café in town.

Living in town was noisy, and keeping a big house was extra work. But Rose had come to like being a town girl. There was always some excitement, and friends close by.

Even though they lived in town now, Papa drove the wagon out to the farm as often as he could, when he wasn't busy hauling freight to and from the depot, or delivering coal oil for Mr. Waters. Mama and Rose went along sometimes to help tend the young apple orchard, which would come into bearing for the first time next fall.

They helped Effie with the garden and helped Abe and Nate in the fields. Soon—as soon as the orchard showed a profit—Mama and Papa planned to move back. "We are farmers, first and last," Mama always said.

The Bairds arrived to supper first, and suddenly the house exploded with laughter and warmth. Rose helped Nate unbundle the babies, who wanted to scamper about and touch everything. They had to watch that James and Elza didn't pull the tassels off the parlor furniture, or climb up on the dining-room chairs to play with the table settings, or get too close to the heater stove.

Effie had brought a crock of hoppin' John, which was black-eyed peas with hog jowl.

"Well, thank you!" Mama said. "Let me put this right on to warm." Abe and Effie followed her and Papa into the kitchen. Rose picked up James, and Nate picked up Elza and tagged along. The babies were getting to be so big, and squirmy, too.

Effie pulled off her bonnet and let down her braid of blond hair. "It ain't for tonight," she declared, as Abe helped her out of her coat. "It's for you'uns to have for your New Year's Day dinner tomorrow. Got to eat hoppin' John for New Year's Day dinner."

"Whatever for?" asked Mama, chuckling as she glanced at Abe. He winked and shrugged as Papa took his coat and hat. Mama took Effie's coat and handed it to Rose to hang on the hall tree in the parlor. But Rose waited to hear.

"It's for good luck," Effie said. "My folks

done it, and the grandfolks, too. On New Year's you jest eat black-eyed peas, and stick a penny under your plate, an' wear a pair of red garters, too. That way you got good luck a-coming in the new year."

Rose guffawed, then clapped a hand over her mouth. Garters were underclothing, to hold up a lady's stockings. A person didn't discuss underclothing in mixed company.

Mama glared at Rose for just an instant, but Rose could see in her eyes a glint of mirth. Effie was very superstitious. She was always telling them about signs and omens.

"Well, then, black-eyed peas it is," said Papa heartily, his mustache twitching. "Why tempt fate, I always say."

"And don't be a-taking nary thing out the house tomorrow," Effie said. "Nary stick of wood nor bucket of ashes. It's terrible bad luck iffen you do. And something else—"

"Now hold your horses, Effie," Abe interrupted. He took her elbow and guided her into the dining room. "You're a-scaring these folks with all your flapdoodle. Quit picking 'round the edges of the world, and come set yourself down. Ain't nothing bad a-going to happen here tonight."

Supper was wonderful and noisy. The savory oyster stew, with its yellow specks of melted butter floating on top and the dark oysters hiding on the bottom, tasted rich and smooth. And there was lots of sleek butter to slather on the still-warm bread. The sounds of firecrackers and shotguns peppered their chatter.

Rose helped Mama clear away the dishes. She was carrying a tray of coffee cups to the table when Effie suddenly jumped up from her chair and cried out, "Grab the littl'uns, Abe. Hit's a shake a-coming!" Rose nearly dropped her tray.

Everyone stopped what they were doing in midair, stopped what they were saying in mid sentence. They all stared open-mouthed at Effie as if she had gone mad.

Poor Effie looked around her, bewildered and frightened. James giggled once from Mrs. Cooley's lap. A passing locomotive tooted its whistle, and then everyone but Effie burst out laughing.

"That's no earthquake, Mrs. Baird. It's just the train," Paul said as the windows rattled in their frames. "You know, it always shakes the houses some."

Effie blushed hard and sat back down.

"You're as jumpy tonight as a long-tailed cat in a roomful of rocking chairs," Papa joshed her, pushing back from the table. "I believe I've just the cure."

He disappeared through the kitchen into the bedroom. He came back with a small bottle filled with amber-colored liquid, and five clean glasses.

"Manly, it's Sunday!" Mama scolded. Papa's proper name was Almanzo, but Mama called him Manly.

"I guess I know what day it is, Bess," Papa said, pulling the cork with a hollow little *thunk*. Mama's proper name was Laura, but Papa called her Bess, which was short for her middle name, Elizabeth.

"I also know it's the last day of the nineteenth century, and something to crow about. I reckon the Lord's got his hands full with sinners tonight. He won't mind if some honest, hardworking folks have a nip of brandy to celebrate."

Mama frowned at him, but when he poured a little of the golden brandy in each glass, and handed one to her, she took it.

"I suppose if everyone is, I might as well," she said shyly. She held it in both hands and waited until all the other grown-ups had theirs.

Rose stared at Mama. She had never, ever seen Mama drink brandy. Once Mama had taken some hard cider, after a day of rendering at one of Mr. Stubbins' hog killings. But Mr. Stubbins was Effie's father, and that was out on the farm, away from the proper manners and prying eyes of town folks. Rose had never seen any woman in town have a drink.

Papa sometimes stopped at the saloon to have a beer after he finished his work. Many of the men in town did, and the women often complained of it: "A man takes a drink, and then the drink takes the man."

The saloon was a wicked place, they all said. No proper woman would ever think to go in there, or walk to the depot by herself. Even if she were going to take a train, a reputable woman found a reputable man—her husband if she had one, or her father if she didn't—to escort her there and see her safely onto the train.

Mama forbade Rose even to walk near the corner of the square where the saloon stood, across from the depot. Some of those men were rough, and on Saturday nights Sheriff Lockwood sometimes had to arrest a drunk or two for fighting. Papa said the sheriff had the right name for the job.

Rose had sneaked to the depot a few times, standing at the end of the platform where she wouldn't be noticed. She loved the commotion that surrounded the panting, steaming trains, the way the people hurried about, their eyes full of purpose and mystery. Boxes and barrels and trunks and grips containing more mysteries littered the platform.

From the depot she had seen men stumble out of the saloon, squinting against the sunlight, their hats askew. She saw the frowns of disapproval on the faces of the women who were waiting to board the cars, and saw them turn away their faces, and shield the faces of their children.

In the newspapers and magazines, and even in her schoolbook, *McGuffey's Fifth Eclectic Reader,* she found writings against the evils of alcohol. They told stories of poor mothers and children left to starve when husbands and fathers became slaves to drink.

But drink never took Papa. He did most of his socializing with the other men in town at the barbershop. Even when he did stop for a beer, he was always the same: good-humored and hardworking. When Mama complained about fighting at the saloon, he said, "Aw, Bess. You know as well as me, all the important men in town go there. Most times it's just a sociable place to sit and chew the fat or play a game of pool. No harm in that."

Mama never scolded him for stopping at the saloon now and then, although she said any town would be better off without one.

To see Mama, Mrs. Cooley, and Effie with their glasses of brandy struck Rose as wonderfully naughty. Women must always keep up their good names, always be sweet and pure. They must be good cooks and tidy housekeepers and dutiful mothers and wives.

And how many times had she heard the older girls at school recite that saying: "Lips that touch liquor will never touch mine."

Of course, men had their reputations to keep, too. A man's word was everything. He must be strong and faithful and dependable, a good provider. But a man could still smoke a cigar and have a drink in a saloon without losing his reputation. He could go to the depot anytime he wished, just to watch the trains come and go. Even boys could do that.

When she was little, Rose thought it would be more fun to be a boy than a girl. Now she knew it was easier to be a man than a woman.

And she was beginning to wonder why that must be so.

Paul, George, and Nate eagerly eyed those golden glasses of brandy. Rose wanted to try a sip too, but none of them dared to ask.

Papa held up his glass and made a toast: "To the next hundred years. May they bring health and prosperity to us all."

"Land sakes, I hope I'm not going to live that long," Mama said. Everyone laughed, and then the five grown-ups all took a dainty little sip and wished each other a happy New Year.

After the table had been cleared and the dishes washed, everyone went into the parlor, and Abe got out his fiddle. Little James clapped his hands with delight, ran to Abe's knee, and hugged it.

Rose could never see that fiddle without thinking of her grandpa Ingalls, Mama's father, far, far away in South Dakota. It had been five and a half years since they left Mama's family behind to move to Missouri. Grandpa was a fiddler too, and Mama often spoke of how she missed the music he played when she was a little girl. His fiddling was something Mama especially liked about Abe. They all did.

The three families sat politely while Abe played two songs that Mama had taught him, "Buffalo Gals" and "The Girl I Left Behind Me." Grandpa Ingalls had played and sung them when Mama was small.

When he finished, Abe put the fiddle down and rubbed fresh rosin on the bow. He shot a sidelong glance at Effie, sitting next to him on the tête-à-tête. "What say we roll back that rug, and I'll teach you folks an old dance step or two."

"Abe Baird!" Effie said, giving him a playful slap on the shoulder. "A-dancing on Sunday! What would the preacher say?"

"Pshaw!" Abe snorted. "The whole durn world's a-dancing tonight. Now ever'body pick a partner. This here's a play-party dance. Pick a partner, now, and make a big circle."

For an instant, Rose hesitated. Her eyes snagged on Nate, who looked at her bashfully. Then she jumped up from her seat and, quick as a wink, grabbed Paul's hand.

She so surprised herself with her boldness that her neck flushed hot with shame. She glanced at Nate and shrugged sheepishly. His forehead creased, and he looked away. She felt a quick beat of remorse, then shrugged it off.

Paul's palm felt so warm, and his long fingers gripped her hand firmly. She had never held his hand before, and there was a guilty pleasure in it. Paul gave her a warm, shy smile, and she basked in its glow.

Mama had taken Papa's hand, and Mrs. Cooley held George's. That left poor Nate to dance with Effie. He made a sour face as he and Effie rolled up the ingrain carpet to one end of the parlor. Then all the dancers joined hands in a circle.

Abe stood by the door, the fiddle cradled under his chin, and called out the steps: "Mr. and Mrs. Wilder, jump in the middle. Pick a boy now, and skip to my Lou."

Mama and Papa stepped into the circle and picked Nate. Then Abe's fiddle began a lively rasping tune as they skipped around the circle, and he sang,

> "*Bugs in the biscuits, two by two,*
> *Bugs in the biscuits, two by two,*
> *Bugs in the biscuits, two by two,*
> *Skip to my Lou, my darlin'.*"

James and Elza chirped with glee, and they danced their own little jumping jig. The floorboards let out little joyful squeaks as Mama and Papa skipped around the little circle with Nate stumbling along between them and giggling.

Mama's cheeks glowed, and her wide violet eyes sparkled like a summer day. Her braid of roan-colored hair, wound into a bun on the back of her head, bounced merrily. Her navy velvet dress flared and twirled with each turn, showing little glimpses of her ankles. Mama would never do that with anyone but the Bairds. A lady never let her ankles show.

Papa looked a bit clumsy, trying to skip. But

he put his head back and roared at Abe's lyrics:

"Hair in the butter, six foot long,
Hair in the butter, six foot long,
Hair in the butter, six foot long,
Skip to my Lou, my darlin'."

Mama and Papa stopped and made an arch with their hands. Nate skipped through it. Then Mama and Papa joined the circle and Nate chose another couple, Mrs. Cooley and George.

"Chicken in the bread pan,
     scratchin' out dough,
Chicken in the bread pan,
     scratchin' out dough,
Chicken in the bread pan,
     scratchin' out dough,
Skip to my Lou, my darlin'."

When Nate picked Rose and Paul to be the next couple, the three of them skipped in

45

perfect time. Rose watched Paul's feet, and Nate watched Rose's and held tight to her hand.

Abe taught them another dance, and then the clock in the dining room struck ten.

"Look at the time!" Mama cried out. "We'd better hurry if we're to make church in time."

The Earth Abideth Forever

I t was odd and exciting to bundle up to go out so late at night. When they lived on the farm, Rose and Mama and Papa always went to bed by eight o'clock. A farmer's day started long before sunup. In town they stayed up a little bit later, perhaps nine o'clock, and a little bit later still in summer when the days were longest.

In their heavy coats and mittens and fascinators they walked through the crisp dark night. A canopy of stars glittered overhead. The town square glowed with light from every store window and from torches that flickered in the still, chilly air. The street was empty of wagons and horses. They had been hitched outside of town, away from the depot where the fireworks might scare them into bolting.

Reverend Mays did not keep the congregation in their pews until midnight. He preached a short service that was made shorter by all the noise. He read a chapter from Ecclesiastes, about the vanity of human wisdom. It was hard to concentrate on the words with the sound of cornets drifting in from the square. The Mansfield band, the Cyclones, had started to play.

But Rose heard two verses that stuck in her mind:

"One generation passeth away, and another generation cometh: but the earth abideth for ever."

Rose thought about that as Reverend Mays plowed on through the "hath"s, the "goeth"s, and the "turneth"s. There had been nineteen new centuries since Christ was born, and how many new centuries before that? More than anyone could count, probably. The living things of the earth—the foolish and the wise—were born, lived, and died, over and over again. But the earth just kept going on, heedless of crop prices or weather. The earth never got lonely, or felt sad, or worried about the future. The earth had no vanity about itself.

All the praying and wars and hard work of people couldn't stop the sun from rising and setting. It always had, and it always would. The clouds would never run out of rain, the rivers would run for eternity, yet the sea would never overflow. Long after all the people in that church had returned to dust, the earth would still be there. It was true, what the Bible said. There *was* nothing new under the sun.

Then Reverend Mays reached the last verse:

"For in much wisdom is much grief: and he that increaseth knowledge increaseth sorrow."

Rose knew that verse was true as well. She didn't even have to think about it. She felt it in her heart.

Just as Reverend Mays closed his Bible, a burst of firecrackers exploded outside the window. Several women cried out in fright. Some of the boys sprang to their feet and stood on tiptoe to look out the dark windows. The bigger girls and the little children tittered nervously. The men covered their mouths with their hands and chuckled, and the women looked at each other with disapproving frowns on their faces.

When the commotion died down, they could hear from outside the low, sniggering laughter of boys. Mr. Gaskill, the postmaster, jumped up and dashed down the aisle, toward the door.

"Hold on there a spell, Noah," Reverend Mays called out. Mr. Gaskill stopped.

"We all know the Lord works in a mysterious way," Reverend Mays said, smiling. "By the sound of the racket out there, I'd say we've done our job and he must be close at hand," he joked. Everyone laughed. "No sense trying to fight nature on a night such as this. Might as well end up with a short prayer and get on with the fun."

Then everyone bundled up again and hurried to the square. The children dashed ahead down the icy street, shrieking with delight. The grown-ups tried to call them back, and then gave up. No amount of scolding could stop their legs from running. They were as determined as moths rushing toward a flame.

The rest of that night was a blur of excitement. Rose and Nate and George left the grown-ups and the twins behind and ran up the stairs to the Opera House. Paul had gone to the depot to talk to Mr. Nickles and to hear all the latest news from the wires.

The Opera House, hazy with coal-oil smoke, was jammed with people. They were sipping lemonade, drinking coffee to warm themselves, and tasting all the cakes and pies and cookies.

The children grabbed a handful of cookies

each and then dashed back down into the square. The Cyclones, in their beautiful green uniforms and caps decorated with gold braid, stood on the high platform of the gazebo in the middle of the square. They played stirring marches and some new love songs. Rose had learned the words to these songs from Blanche, and she sang along as they walked around the square, nibbling ginger cookies and watching the young men throw scraps of wood and excelsior on the soaring pillar of barrels that would soon be set afire.

> *"Daisy, Daisy, give me your answer true.*
> *I'm half crazy, all for the love of you!*
> *It won't be a stylish marriage,*
> *I can't afford a carriage,*
> *But you'll look sweet*
> *Upon the seat*
> *Of a bicycle built for two!"*

At one corner of the square, a group of men and women prayed with all their might. Their loose rumpled clothing and muddy boots told

Rose they were farmers, not from town. A preacher holding a Bible shook it and beat it with his fist. He cried out over the blare of music and the hum of the swarming crowd.

"The world's gone puny with sin, and the breath of the Devil is a-coming, a-breathing fire out the blackness of the earth! Is you ready to go with the Lord? Is you ready for the storm?"

"Amen," the farmers shouted back. "We're ready! Bring on the Judgment Day!"

"That preacher's lost the buttons on his britches," said Nate.

"They must be Earthquake Christians," guessed Rose.

Finally the Cyclones stopped playing, and someone began beating the fire bell to count down the last seconds. The three children ran to the top of the square, near the barrel pile. Some men were pouring coal oil on it.

"Twenty, nineteen, eighteen, seventeen . . . ," the crowd shouted all together and surged toward the depot. Everywhere men had their pocket watches out. The blood rushed to Rose's head, and her heart fluttered. Mama, Papa, Mrs. Cooley, and the Bairds had come up behind her. She looked for Paul, but he was nowhere to be seen.

"Ten, nine, eight . . ." Nate grabbed Rose's shoulders from behind and shook her. "It's the quake!" he shouted. Rose screamed with delight. George did a cartwheel.

"Three, two, one . . ." the crowd roared. Then everything in town that could began to make noise. "Happy New Year!" the people shouted, and everywhere folks hugged each other. Others beat on old washpans and buckets. The whistles at the sawmill and the flour mill began to shriek. The bells on the churches clanged.

Several boys tossed torches on the barrel pile, and it burst into flames. Then three rockets *whoompf*ed on the other side of the railroad tracks. A trail of sparks followed each one as it soared high into the black night sky, *kaboom!* The crowd *ooh*ed and *aah*ed with pleasure.

A huge, deafening blast shook the whole town, so loud Rose felt her insides shudder. Someone at the livery stable had shot off an anvil.

Now more rockets went up, exploding into flowers and fountains of dazzling colored lights. The Cyclones began to play, this time "*Stars and Stripes Forever.*" The pile of barrels quickly became a roaring pillar of flame that lit the whole square as bright as noon, as hot as a kitchen stove. Rose felt her face grow warm.

Suddenly Paul's grinning face appeared in front of her. He grabbed her by the shoulders and hugged her hard. He shouted something she couldn't understand at first.

"My first assignment! Isn't it swell?" Paul cried out. She had never seen him so stirred up.

"What?" Rose nearly had to scream to make herself heard. "An assignment?"

"It just came in, over the wire. Mr. Nickles arranged it all!" He shoved a telegram in her hand, but in her confusion, and the dim light, the writing on the paper looked only like chicken scratches.

"They're holding a position, in Grinnell!" Paul crowed, his eyes shining fiercely. "When I'm done school this spring. I'm going to be a telegrapher, Rose. It's for certain now. I'm really going to be one!"

"Oh, Paul, it's wonderful!" Rose said. She flinched as another anvil shot off at the livery stable. "Where's Grinnell?"

"Gosh, I dunno. I think he said it's Iowa. Yup, Iowa."

She stared at Paul in stunned disbelief. Iowa!

"But how . . . when . . . ," Rose stammered.

"I'll be moving up there, soon's school's done," Paul said. The words tumbled out as fast as he could speak them. "But sometimes, now and then, I can come home for a visit. It's good pay, too. I can send most of it to Mother, and still have enough to live. Course I'll start on the night shift, and it's a small depot. Not many train orders. But, in time . . ."

Rose did not hear another word. Louder than any anvil, as shattering as any earthquake, the word "Iowa" exploded in her mind. Her chest tightened, and she had to fight for her breath. Paul was moving away. He was leaving town.

Conscious Pride

Rose handed Effie a clean damp cloth and set the small crock of skunk grease on a chair where she could reach it. Effie dabbed up a bit of the grease on the cloth. Then she reached under her bedcovers to rub it on her chest.

Rose wrinkled her nose against the searing fumes. The stale odor of sickness lingered in that room in the farmhouse like a thick, unpleasant fog.

Effie smiled weakly. "Don't smell too good, do it?" Her burning fever had broken, and the natural pink had come back in her cheeks. But she still wheezed when she breathed, and her nose ran like a spring.

"It's horrible," said Rose. "I wouldn't wear any, even if I was deathly sick. Why do you do it?"

Effie let out a small chuckle that ended in a cough. Only two weeks into the new year she'd been struck down by the grippe. Rose had come out to Rocky Ridge Farm to sit with Effie and take care of the twins while Abe and Nate did the farm chores. Mrs. Stubbins, Effie's mother, had taken a turn, and so had Mama. Now Rose was giving them a rest.

"When I was a littl'un and a-feeling mighty puny, Ma always made me to wear it. I cried something awful, it stank so bad. But it always fixed me up right, in the end."

Rose put the lid back on the crock and took it outside on the porch where the grease would stay solid and not smell the house up any worse. The weather had turned dreadfully cold. One night the thermometer in the kitchen showed thirty degrees below zero. All the creeks froze solid, and in the morning when Rose went to pump water from the well at the house in town, her hand stuck to the metal handle. Mama had to pour warm water on it to get her free.

The long dreary weeks of midwinter had begun. The wind had blown the last dead leaves from the trees, robbing the farm of its leafy dress. The shabby secrets of everyday living stared her bleakly in the face. The barns, the privy, the henhouse, the wood and manure piles all stood exposed and ugly.

She shivered against the icy wind and hurried back inside. She dropped the soiled cloth into a bucket of soapy water by the stove. Then she poured Effie a fresh cup of yellow-root tea and checked the twins. They slept peacefully in their trundle beds, which had been moved into the kitchen until Effie was mended.

Being in that little house, where she had lived before they moved to town, always felt odd to Rose. It was a museum of remembered moments. She thought about the life she had now, against her life as a farm girl. When she saw the henhouse full of chickens needing to be fed and watered every day, and the spring where water must be hauled in heavy buckets up the steep bank, and the muddy footprints on the kitchen floor needing to be scrubbed, she knew she liked living in town.

She felt guilty about that, the way a person remembers a half-done chore left for someone else to finish. She loved the farm, its peacefulness and the pleasure of caring for the livestock, and making the garden grow. But she was older now. She wouldn't want to give up the swirl and excitement of town life for anything. It was selfish, but she couldn't help feeling that way.

The ringing of Abe's axe echoed from the woodlot. He and Nate were cutting a load of firewood to sell. A redbird flashed by the window.

"Fetch me my brush, Rose. I might fix my hair some," Effie said, pulling herself up a bit. "I hate it for Abe to see me in such a state."

Rose plumped up her pillows. As she moved them, she spotted a wooden handle underneath. She shifted the pillows and saw the glint of a butcher-knife blade.

"Effie, what in the world . . . ?"

"Oh, that." She chuckled. "It's for to keep away the bad dreams. My little sister, Alva, she used to wake up a-hollering ever' night. But Ma put a knife under her pillow, and she had nary trouble after that."

She pulled a hank of her long blond hair across her chest and began working at the tangles.

"I been a-dreaming up a storm since I got my fever. I was a-dreaming Abe and me was a-driving in a buggy with a team of white horses. That's a bad sign, but it come a mite late," she said, pulling at a tangle.

"White horses is a bad omen?" asked Rose. She perched on the chair by the bed and drew up one leg so she could rest her chin on her knee.

"To dream of 'em means sickness is a-coming. But I was sick already."

"I dreamed of a horse," Rose suddenly remembered. "Just the other night."

"Hope it weren't no white one," Effie said, frowning.

"No, it was an ordinary horse, a Morgan mare I think, like Papa's. I was bringing home a sack of flour from town, and I stopped to pick some daisies. But when I went to put the sack back on the horse, she trotted a little way off and stopped to nibble some grass. Each time I got close enough to almost catch her, she ran ahead. I chased that ornery horse over the hills and through the hollows. But I never could catch her. Then I woke up so mad."

Effie picked up her cup, blew on the bitter tea, and took a sip, humming thoughtfully. "I'm a-studying on it, and I reckon it's a dream about a body a-going away. Maybe you're a-going to travel, Rose."

Rose shook her head, but then she remembered something else. "Paul is going away," she said mournfully. "He has a position waiting for him, in Iowa. He's going to be a telegrapher, when school is finished."

Effie raised an eyebrow. "You ain't sweet on Paul now, is you?"

"Oh, no!" Rose lied earnestly. She felt her face grow warm. She gazed into her lap and picked at a loose thread. "I just . . . well, Paul is . . . I mean we grew up together, since we were little. And Mrs. Cooley, being a widow and all. Why, she even cried when he told her. And George such a vexing boy to take care of all by herself."

She balled her hands into fists and plopped them in her lap in exasperation. "It's just a shame he couldn't find a position right here in Mansfield. Paul's in such a hurry to make his way. Why couldn't he wait?"

Effie coughed and set down her cup. "I reckon he's skittish like that old dream horse of yourn. You oughtn't to fret so, Rose. A horse always finds its way back to the stable."

Rose sighed. The new century hadn't started off any way she'd expected. Ever since Paul had told her he would be leaving town, she'd felt such a heaviness in her soul, as though a rock had gotten stuck in her heart. She dreaded the end of school in two months, when Paul would board a train to go to Grinnell.

Just before supper Mrs. Stubbins came to stay. Rose walked back to town under a dark gray sky, shoulders hunched against the gathering night, thinking about her dream. She stopped for a moment to listen to an owl hooting somewhere down along Fry Creek.

Rose had wished for a long time to be older, hoping Paul would notice her in some special way. Now she finally was getting older, and Paul was drifting off. When the two families visited, he wasn't interested anymore in a game of checkers, or a walk to the square. Right away he wanted to sit in the parlor and talk with Papa about the big changes coming in the country.

"That boy's smart as a whip," Papa said. "He can hold his own against any man debating if McKinley'll take another term for president, or if bimetallism is a good thing for the country."

"What's bimetallism?" Rose wondered.

"The silver issue," said Papa. "It's difficult to explain. You wouldn't care about it. But that Paul, he's got a head on his shoulders."

Rose really didn't care about bimetallism, but she wished she did.

Overnight Paul seemed to have grown taller, too. At school he swaggered manfully, bragged to the other boys, and hardly spoke two words to her. He was a young man now, and that made Rose feel as invisible as a little girl.

There was Nate to think of, too. Lately he had been coming by every chance he could, wanting to talk about his adventure books, or to boast of beating some other boy in mumblety-peg. In the schoolyard at recess, when he spotted Rose he'd show off by doing a flip or knocking off someone's hat.

He had started coming to the Methodist Church every Sunday, instead of going to the country church Abe and Effie attended. He sat with the smirking boys in the back pews, rustling stealthily. When the congregation stood to sing, he and the other boys sneaked out the door to stand around outside and watch the older boys smoke cigars and tell their awful jokes.

One Sunday after church, Nate stepped out of the crowd of young men who always waited by the walk to watch the young ladies come out, hoping one of them would let them walk her home.

Nate stole a sideways glance at Rose and mumbled, "See ya home?"

Before she could stop herself, Rose let out a laugh. "Nate Baird!" she chortled in a voice so flippant and cutting even she blushed to hear it. "Have you gone feather-brained? I always walk home with Mama and Papa and the Cooleys."

"Aw, I was just joshing," Nate muttered, kneading his hat in his hands, then jamming it back on his head. His big ears turned bright pink. "Just to see what you'd say."

"Well, I would say I'm not even in long skirts yet and after all, you're most nearly a brother. And brothers don't see their own sisters home from church, do they? I don't know what's gotten into you lately. Come along now, if you want to stay to dinner."

Then she flounced off down the walk, leaving poor Nate to stare red-faced at his shoes.

Rose scolded herself for being pitiless. It was plain as pudding that Nate liked her. But she could never think of him as a beau, any more than she could think of flying onto a tree branch and singing like a wren. In her eyes, Nate was still a little boy.

Rose found no joy in school, either. Professor Bland's lessons bored her. Rose had always been ahead of the other scholars in her studies. She read every moment she could, and devoured long grown-up books. Mama had given her lessons at home, in ciphering and geography and history. She knew there was nothing Professor Bland could teach her that she didn't already know.

She could not hide her true feelings, and Professor Bland often had to scold her. One day he gave a lesson in transposition. He read aloud some lines of poetry by Alfred, Lord

Tennyson. Mama had a whole book of Tennyson's poems. At night after supper she sometimes read her favorites aloud to Rose and Papa, and Rose had read all the rest on her own. Rose even knew some of them by heart.

> "*Break, break, break!*
> *On the cold gray stones, O sea,*"

Professor Bland read. Rose whispered the words before he could say them as she sat at her desk drawing a picture of a cat on a blank page in her reader.

> "*And I would that I could utter the*
> *thoughts that arise in me.*"

There was a long silence. Rose looked up. Professor Bland was leaning on his desk, glaring at her from under his dark brows.

"Miss Wilder, as you seem to be familiar with this verse, favor us with your transposition of these lines," he demanded. "Tell us what they mean."

Rose laid down her pencil and stood. "They don't mean anything," she declared peevishly. A nervous titter ran through the room.

"Surely they mean something," Professor Bland insisted, staring hard and tapping his ruler on his desk.

"It is poetry," Rose said. "It can't be transposed. What it means is not what it says."

He grunted, "Humpf!" As he stalked down a row of desks, he caught Jessie Gaskill reading a note. He snatched it away, read it, and crumpled it up in his fist.

"Sit down, Miss Wilder. Let us see if some other scholar understands these lines." Rose sat, fuming. "Oscar Hensley, stand and transpose."

Oscar stood and proudly said, "Smash on your rocks, O Ocean, and I wish that I could say what I think about it."

Now Professor Bland sauntered down the aisle to the desk Rose shared with Cora Hibbard. Cora shrank away as he looked down at the cat in Rose's book.

"Let this be a lesson to you," he said sharply, tapping the end of his ruler on her book. Rose refused to look up. She took her pencil and furiously scribbled a tail on her cat.

"You fail because you do not try. You see that Oscar succeeds in doing what you would not attempt. Perseverance is the chief virtue. Without it you will accomplish nothing in life. If at first you don't succeed, you must not weakly give up. You must—"

Rose could not bear another word. She threw down her pencil and slammed her book shut. She gathered her things, jumped up, and went to fetch her coat from the cloakroom. Then she stormed out the door, Professor Bland's words trailing her down the stairs, "You see, children, that pride is at the bottom of all mistakes."

"However will you get on in this world if you fly off at the smallest hitch?" Mama complained. "I ought to send you straight back there, to apologize."

Rose sighed, but she knew Mama wouldn't.

She could be strict, and she certainly was old-fashioned in many ways. But when it came to lessons, she and Rose thought the same way: "Better to stand alone in conscious pride than err with millions on your side."

"I do wish at the least you might learn to suffer quietly," Mama pleaded from her rocking chair in the dining room. Her needle stabbed at her sewing. "I don't believe Professor Bland is so terrible you couldn't try to be polite."

Rose set her book and slate down on the dining table. "He's boring," she groused. "And he nags me for speaking my own thoughts. Professor Blah-Blah-Blah."

A laugh jerked from Mama's throat, and Rose herself couldn't stifle a chuckle.

"Very well, then. If you're going to stay at home, you can finish piecing together your new lawn. Warm weather'll be here before you know it. After that, we'll work some on your ciphering. But first fetch some wood for the heater stove. I feel a chill from the window."

Rose sat at the dining table sewing whipstitches. Mama sat still in her rocker, her work-chafed hands sewing a new collar to one of Papa's work shirts. Concentration ridged her forehead, and she squinted through her new eye glasses, which made her beautiful large eyes look even wider.

Strong afternoon light poured through the frost-covered window behind Mama's rocker. It lit her hair, highlighting the strands of gray that had begun to show near the part in the middle. In her Mother Hubbard, hunched over her work, Mama looked so small and careworn. A wave of pity washed over Rose and quickly changed to remorse at the worry she caused Mama by her stubbornness.

She had been rude to Professor Bland, and now Mama must listen to his complaint the next time she saw him. It had been that way almost every school session since they moved to the Ozarks. Rose mostly disliked her teachers, except Mrs. Honeycutt in the Fourth Reader. She was kind and patient and even played with the scholars at recess.

Every year Rose started the session full of

hope, and partway through every year, except for Mrs. Honeycutt, she would quit in a fit of boredom. It was one thing Mama always forgave. Rose was so far ahead of the other children, and Mama herself had taken many of her lessons at home when she was a girl. Besides, the house and farm could always do with an extra pair of hands.

Thinking about her frustration at school, thinking about Paul, and Nate, and all the other burdens of her young heart, Rose found little in her life to make her smile.

Miss Sarah

With Nate always showing off, and Paul drifting away, Rose began to pass more of her time with Blanche Coday. Blanche was fourteen, a year older than she. They had been friends ever since the time Rose beat Blanche to win a spell-down, in Professor Kay's Third Reader class.

Of course, Rose had little free time for anything but the chores that kept her busy at home. Sunday was the only day she had some hours to herself, and that was mostly in the afternoon.

Blanche lived such a different life. She had

no housework, or none to speak of. Edwinna, the hired girl, did most of the housework, and Blanche had brothers to do the heavy work and keep the woodbox full. Rose envied her ease and freedom. Mrs. Coday was not so strict as Mama, so Blanche was always out gadding about town.

Sometimes, in good weather, they would go for a walk to the square, and Rose began to go with Blanche to the second service at Prairie Hollow Church, on Sunday evenings. Mama fussed about that, at first.

"And what's wrong with our church of a sudden? You said you liked Reverend Mays' sermons." But when Rose complained that she hardly had time to visit with Blanche, and anyway she didn't need to hear Reverend Mays twice in the same day, Mama let Rose go, with a warning to come straight home after.

The two girls sometimes visited at the Codays' beautiful house, never at Rose's. Mama said she ought at least to ask Blanche in to supper now and then. "It's simple good manners to return an act of hospitality. You don't want to become beholden to folks."

"Yes, Mama. I will," Rose said. But she never did. The modesty, the commonness, of her life at home embarrassed her. Why would Blanche ever want to sit and look at magazines in their plain parlor, with its bleached muslin curtains and worn secondhand carpet? In her own beautiful home, Edwinna would serve them lemon cookies and tea, and Blanche had a real bedroom with lace curtains, not an attic crawl space like Rose's that a person could hardly stand up in.

Rose understood that her family wasn't quite poor. They were better than that. They had the farm, and the house in town. There was always enough to eat and money for shoes and piece goods to sew up their clothing.

But they did need the extra cash money that boarders brought, and that meant more people to cook and clean for. They had extra bedrooms in that house, and the two dollars a week Mama got for bed and board was nothing to sneeze at, even with her eggs getting twelve cents the dozen.

It was true that they owned the house in town, and Papa owned his wagon and the finest pair of Morgan horses anyone could want. They had the cow and her calf, the chickens, and a pair of mules that stayed out on the farm.

But Papa could never make enough for them all just from driving the draywagon, and delivering coal oil for Mr. Waters' company. Besides the everyday costs, there were taxes to pay and the farm mortgage to be kept up. That was almost more important than food on the table.

Miss Sarah Bates, the schoolteacher, had been boarding at the Helfinstines', up the street near the edge of town. But Mr. Helfinstine's old mother, who had consumption, had come from Kansas to live with them. They needed the room, so Miss Sarah had come to board with the Wilders.

Miss Sarah was an old maid. Once, when they first moved to town two years before,

Blanche had told Rose about her. Blanche had said people should feel sorry for old maids, and then she'd sung a mean ditty about old maids. Now Miss Sarah had come to live with Rose's family. Rose was curious to see if she would feel sorry for Miss Sarah, too.

Miss Sarah did not look like an old maid. She had thick fair hair, coiled in braids. She had blue eyes and a beautifully curved, firm mouth. She moved with a kind of cozy awkwardness, but she was neat and, in a modest way, stylish. She was very polite, although when she spoke to Rose she used her schoolteacher voice.

One day, when Mrs. Cooley came by to work on a quilt with Mama, Rose overheard them speaking about her.

"She must have been pretty as a girl," Mama said. "Why nobody ever took a shine to her beats me."

Mrs. Cooley murmured in agreement. "Well, now you point it out, she's thrifty and capable, too. And a good cook. Yes, she'd've made a real helpmeet for some good man."

"I declare," Mama said through the thread clenched in her teeth. "When you see the girls that do get married, seems to me men haven't the sense that God gave little apples."

Miss Sarah was twenty-six years old and had never had a beau that anyone knew of. She had taught school since she was sixteen, at first in country schools and now at Rose's school in town.

She gave good satisfaction to the school board, and Blanche's father, who was president, said she could go right on teaching Primer and First Readers as long as she lived. Her wages were thirty dollars a month, eight months of every year, so she was provided for and could save something for her old age.

Her parents were dead, and she had no relatives to take her in. Rose felt sorry for that. Boarding with the Helfinstines, and now with Rose's family, she could lead a respectable life and keep up her good reputation.

Miss Sarah made no bones about being an old maid. She did not dress in a kittenish way or pretend to be younger than she was.

Whenever she was with the married women, when Mama had a quilting at the house, or a meeting of the Eastern Star ladies, she always said right out that she was an old maid.

When one of the married women would pass a complaint across the quilting frame about her husband's cigar smoking, Miss Sarah would say, "Of course, I couldn't pretend to know about that. I'm only an old maid." Sometimes she would help Rose and Mama cook, and when Papa complimented her on it, she would say, "I guess it's as good as can be expected from an old maid with no husband to practice on." When Mama said how well her cashmere dress was wearing, five years old and still good as new, she'd answer, "Well, I try to look as well as the Lord'll let me, for all I'm an old maid."

She flushed a little when she said these things, and her voice had a hard cheeriness. Her eyes fascinated Rose. They were cheerful and hard too, but they widened a little, and waited, as if they were determined to be cheerful no matter what happened.

"Oh, well, Miss Sarah," one of the married women would say awkwardly, "I guess if truth was known, you've had chances." Or, another would say, "We all know you're only waiting for Mr. Right to come along."

Miss Sarah would toss her head and laugh brightly. "Oh, I'm not one to take the first that offers," she'd say, red spots burning on her cheeks. "Just to have 'Mrs.' carved on my tombstone!" All the women stirred uncomfortably.

Rose couldn't understand why Miss Sarah always was saying she was an old maid when she didn't seem to enjoy speaking of it. But she always did. If she'd said nothing, it could be forgotten. Everyone could pretend it made no difference.

Then, one Sunday night at Prairie Hollow Church, something happened that set the whole town talking about Miss Sarah. She had gone to church with the Codays. Being an unmarried woman she couldn't, of course, go to church alone. Because she didn't go to Mama and Papa's church, she usually went with the Helfinstines, but that Sunday they had taken poor old Mrs. Helfinstine to the hospital in Springfield for special treatments.

It was the first mild night telling of the coming spring. The air held the scent of dewy grass and plowed gardens. The streets were muddy, and on the way to church Rose heard the first songs of the spring peepers in the creek that ran by the livery stable. That was one of Rose's favorite sounds, the very first sign that winter would soon be ending.

Rose sat with the Codays and Miss Sarah in the middle of the pews, halfway between the pulpit and the door. In their seats behind the organ, the young ladies of the choir were demure. The old men and women sat on the mourners benches in front with their heads bowed. Behind them were the young ladies with their beaux, and in the back the boys and young men stirred restlessly.

After church, when Rose and Blanche came out into the night and walked down the steps, they craned and pushed and hung back, as they always did, to see the big boys step up to ask the girls, "Can I see you home?" Everything was confused in the crowded darkness. From the door came a shaft of dim lantern light. In the shadows boys were jostling and jeering. Men stopped to light lanterns, and women nudged and murmured.

Rose did not see Wade Tucker step up to Miss Sarah, but she felt the sensation that ran through the crowd. Then, in the gleam of a lantern, she caught sight of Miss Sarah's face, startled, embarrassed, almost frightened. Her gloved hand was on Wade Tucker's arm.

Rose stood in their way, staring up at them, too shocked to move until Blanche's hand jerked her aside. In the silence, Miss Sarah walked down the steps with Wade Tucker.

Everyone began to talk at once.

"Did you ever?" Mrs. Coday breathed.

"Wade Tucker, of all people!" another woman gasped.

He was a bachelor, thirty years old. Papa knew him from the barbershop. Rose had heard him tell Mama that Wade was a great flirt who always bragged that no girl could outsmart him. And no girl ever had.

Rose had seen Wade around town. There was a dash and glitter about him. He wore boiled shirts and stiff collars every day, and a diamond horseshoe pin in his tie. He smoked two-for-a-quarter cigars, and Papa said his stories and jokes were the life of the barbershop.

He drove a wild team in ivory-trimmed harness, on a red-wheeled buggy. People said that with his devil-may-care driving he would kill himself yet.

Old Mr. Tucker was dead. He had been the saloonkeeper and had left Mrs. Tucker and Wade well provided for. Wade did no work. He spent his time playing cards, going to dances, driving fast around the streets, or lounging at the barbershop, dreaming up some prank or other.

Now Miss Sarah had let him walk her home from church. It was almost too fantastic to believe.

Rose and the Codays joined the procession

of groups and couples walking down the slope from church, across the railroad tracks, and along the sidewalk by the square. Here and there men's legs cast long shadow-scissors snipping across a patch of lantern light.

There always was a murmur of talk after church, but that night it was a buzz. Little boys kept racing ahead, waiting in front of Miss Sarah and Wade Tucker, then yelling as they pass by.

"I'd think their mothers'd make them behave," Mrs. Coday said angrily. Rose just stared at the couple's backs, too bewitched by what was happening to say anything, or even to giggle when Blanche poked her in the ribs.

At the corner of the square, where the Codays would turn left to go home, and Rose would turn right, Blanche begged her mother to let her walk Rose home.

Mrs. Coday agreed quickly. Everyone would want to know what might happen when Wade and Miss Sarah reached the gate of Rose's house. So Rose and Blanche followed them down the street, past the livery barn and the stores, across the little bridge, toward her house. The two girls walked in fascinated silence.

In the starlight Rose could see the tilt of Wade's hat, his jaunty shoulders, and sometimes a blur of his face turned toward Miss Sarah. She could see Miss Sarah's straight back and the bunch of her held-up skirts. He was doing most of the talking, but she couldn't hear what he said.

Finally Wade and Miss Sarah reached the gate to Rose's house and stopped. "Keep walking," Rose whispered. "We'll go 'round the back."

Rose felt terribly wicked slinking past the couple on the far side of the street, pretending not to notice but seeing everything, her ears pricked for the faintest sigh. She held her breath and tiptoed, trying to silence the noise of her shoes on the gravel sidewalk.

With a flourish, Wade lifted his hat in a greeting to Mr. Hardesty, who was passing with his family on the way home. The Hardestys lived in the next house east of

Rose's, on the way out of town. Rose heard a door close inside, so she knew Mama and Papa were home. Otherwise she would have run inside and peeked out a parlor window.

Miss Sarah's face was turned a little aside, and she was looking down. After Rose and Blanche passed, they heard her breathless voice say, "Well, I . . . Well, good night, Mr. Tucker."

Wade's voice answered confidently, as if he were laughing a little. When Rose and Blanche reached the alley that ran alongside Rose's house, they turned into it and looked back. The couple were still at the gate. Then the girls ran to the back door, whispering and giggling as loud as they dared.

A Low-Down Trick

The next morning Rose decided she just had to go to school, no matter how awful Professor Bland might be. She simply had to see Blanche again, and gossip about Miss Sarah with the other girls.

At breakfast Miss Sarah was the same as always, quiet and polite. No one dared speak of the night before. It was almost as if Wade's walking her home had been a dream. Nothing had changed, yet the very air seemed to crackle.

Before lessons took up, all the girls in

Rose's class were huddled by the door talking about the night before. They all wanted Rose to tell what had happened.

"Did they kiss?" asked Elsa Beaumont. Her father was the banker, and her older sister, Lois, had tricked Paul Cooley at the pie supper the year before. "Tell the truth, now," Elsa demanded, her eyes dancing with mischief.

"I don't know," Rose answered. "I didn't see it, anyway."

At recess, Rose found Blanche in her Sixth Reader class, and together they went downstairs to Miss Sarah's classroom to peek in the door and look at her.

She was at her desk, surrounded by little girls, and did not seem at all changed to Rose. But she was looking everywhere for her pencil, and she flushed when Blanche called out to her that it was stuck in her hair. Rose stepped back out of the doorway so Miss Sarah wouldn't see her.

Blanche said pertly, "I guess you've got something on your mind, Miss Sarah."

Rose gasped. Blanche could be so bold sometimes.

Miss Sarah's hard voice came out the doorway. "You might have something on yours, miss, if . . ." But Blanche's father was on the school board. So Miss Sarah only said, " . . . if you were teaching thirty young ones."

"She's gone on Wade Tucker, anybody can see she is," Blanche gushed when she and Rose were outside in the schoolyard. "But she'll never land him, never in this world."

They stood watching some little girls skipping rope.

"Well, but he took her home from church," Rose said. "That's sparking as sure as anything, isn't it?"

"I don't care," Blanche insisted. "Mama says there are just as good fish in the sea as ever were caught, and she says Wade Tucker's one of 'em and he always will be."

"Then why'd he see her home?" Rose argued. Now Rose felt sorry for Miss Sarah, to be talked about so. She clung to hope for her.

But at dinner that day, after Miss Sarah had

eaten and gone uptown to the post office, Papa couldn't keep an ashamed grin from his face as he stirred the sugar into his coffee.

"Well, I can tell you why Wade Tucker saw Miss Sarah home last night."

Mama paused on her way to the kitchen with a stack of dirty plates. She shot him a worried look. Rose brushed crumbs off the red-and-white-checked tablecloth.

"Well, why?" she finally asked.

"Jessie Nickles dared him to. And Wade bet Jessie five dollars he'd do it, and kiss her into the bargain."

Mama set the dishes back down on the table with a startling clatter. She flushed hotly and planted her fists on her hips. "I never *heard* of anything so *outrageous*! And you, Manly. Sitting there grinning at it."

Papa forced a sober face, and pulled at his mustache. "I'm not grinning," he said indignantly. "I know it's a low-down mean trick as much as you."

But the grin kept struggling back.

"Only, it was kind of funny," he muttered,

ashamed. "The way Wade got to talking, in the barbershop."

Mama's eyes flashed blue with fury. "Low-down, mean, contemptible trash."

Rose was shocked at Mama's anger and at the horrible trick Wade was playing on poor Miss Sarah. She gathered up the dishes and slunk into the kitchen, where she could hear without being seen.

"How you men can sit around listening to him and laughing! Did he say he kissed her?"

"Well, not exactly," Papa said in a low voice.

"What do you mean, not exactly? He either did or he didn't, didn't he? Well, what are you keeping back now? She's living under our roof, Manly. We have a duty to protect her good name."

Papa's voice went cold sober. "Seems Jessie Nickles and a couple others snuck down through the back lots last night after church, and listened from behind the bushes over at Gaskill's next door. Jessie claims Wade lost the bet. But Wade says he never bet *when* he'd kiss her.

"It's downright mean, for a fact," he admitted. "But Wade raised the bet to twenty-five dollars, and he says he'll kiss her, all right."

Rose heard a chair slam against the table. Then Mama said slowly, "Killing's too good for him. Poor Miss Sarah. Somebody ought to tell her!"

"It's not your affair," Papa said dryly. "Miss Sarah can take well-enough care for herself, I reckon."

Mama came into the kitchen, carrying the coffee cups, her face set in a hard, thoughtful look. Rose helped her wash the dishes in silence, afraid to speak. Mama's forehead stayed furrowed in thought. As they finished drying the last saucer, Rose found the courage to pipe up: "Mama, Miss Sarah's got good sense, doesn't she?"

"Yes," Mama agreed. "She's got good sense. But for all that, she's an old maid, and Wade is a good catch, although money isn't everything. She'll never let him kiss her unless they're engaged. I worry if he goes that far, he'll be expected to marry her. But I don't think he would."

Rose clapped a hand over her mouth. "You don't mean he'd jilt her!"

Mama wiped down the kitchen table and dropped the rag in the washpan.

"He would," she declared. "That's what he'll do, jilt her. And she'll never be able to stay here and face it. She's got too much pride. It's bad enough being an old maid. She tries to carry that off. But if he makes such a laughingstock of her . . . Only she hasn't got anybody or anyone to go to, that I ever heard of."

Then she turned on Rose and looked her right in the eye. "You keep quiet about this, you hear? Remember what I've taught you about gossip. I'll not have a daughter of mine spreading tales."

It frightened Rose to see Miss Sarah's innocence after that. It seemed impossible that she didn't know people had been talking about her. But she did not know, or else she didn't mind it. She laughed and chattered more than before, and with a kind of shy happiness.

After Wade Tucker took her home again the next Sunday after church, Miss Sarah went to Reynolds' Store and bought fourteen yards of foulard. She sewed on the new dress in her room until all hours, and wore it the next Sunday.

The foulard was blue-black, with an overall pattern in shaded grays. She had made it up with mousquetaire sleeves and three graduated flounces trimmed with double ruffles. White ruching edged the boned collar and gave her face a clear, transparent look. Her eyes seemed bluer and her smile more brilliant.

That Sunday, when Miss Sarah walked down the aisle after church, the young men and all the boys at the back of the church were waiting to see what would happen. Wade stood in the aisle letting people go past him. Just as Miss Sarah reached him, he threw his head back and let a laugh silently appear on his face, for everyone to see but her. Miss Sarah's eyes were downcast. She pretended she didn't know he was there.

Then he stepped out jauntily beside her. She glanced at him and took his arm as if in triumph, as if she seemed to be aware of everyone but him. Rose was bewildered. It was almost as if Wade was the one to be sorry for.

Once again, Rose followed them home, then skittered past them standing at the gate of the house in the darkness, and down the alley to the backyard and into the kitchen door. But Mrs. Coday would not let Blanche go with her.

Mama wouldn't let Rose go into the parlor, where she might peek out the window. She kept her in the kitchen and made her tell what had happened at church. Mama clucked with disapproval.

The next day when Rose came home from school for her dinner, Papa and Mama were in the kitchen, and she could hear Papa's voice:

"Well, Wade says they must have stood out there 'til . . ." As soon as Rose opened the door, they both fell suddenly silent. Then Mama changed the subject. "When are we going to get Abe in here to plow up the garden, Manly? I do believe ours'll be the last in town to get turned."

Dinner was awkward again when Miss Sarah came home. It was a terrible strain pretending to ignore the secret that everyone knew. Miss Sarah chattered about something humorous that one of the children had said, and remarked on the fine sunny weather.

When Rose went back to school, she heard from Elsa Beaumont all about what Wade had said at the barbershop that morning. Elsa had overheard Mr. Beaumont telling Mrs. Beaumont.

"Wade called Miss Sarah 'Sweetness,'" Elsa said, her face beaming with vicious amusement. "And he called her 'Cutie.' And she just lapped it up. The men in the barbershop nearly died laughing. And she let him hold her hand."

"She didn't!" Rose cried. "I don't believe it!"

"Mr. Nickles saw her," Elsa declared. "And he tried to kiss her, and she said, 'Oh, Mr. Tucker! You mustn't!'"

Elsa somehow made it seem as funny as the hideous comic Valentines that people sometimes gave.

"I don't think it's funny!" Blanche exclaimed, horrified, laughing.

"You ought to be ashamed, Elsa Beaumont," said Cora Hibbard.

"Well, she ought to have better sense," Elsa said haughtily, playing with her gold bracelet. "She ought to know nobody's going to fall for her at this late date. My goodness, she's twenty-six! But Mama says an old maid'll just believe what a man tells her. If you don't have sense enough to get married, she says, why, then you don't have any better sense than that."

Next Sunday, Miss Sarah wore a new hat. She had sent away to a mail-order house for it. It was a turban of purple pansies, with a purple bow and a clutch of wheat standing up at one side. A chenille-dotted veil came just over the tip of her nose. Her cheeks were flushed all through the service. Wade Tucker saw her home again.

When Rose walked home after school the next day, she found Mama talking to Mrs. Gaskill at the side fence. They had been taking in the washing. Rose came up behind Mama and heard her say, "It's going too far. It's got to be put a stop to."

"Well, she says herself the purple's brighter than she thought it would be, from the catalogue," Mrs. Gaskill murmured. "And now she's got it, of course she's got to wear it out. But Mr. Nickles says Wade says . . ."

Then Mama caught sight of Rose. "You go in the house, and take that school dress off this minute."

When Mama came in with the clean clothes, her eyes were determined and her mouth was a thin line. She took off her apron, smoothed her hair, and put on her second-best hat. Her afternoon calico was clean and neat.

"You peel the potatoes and put them to boil," she said.

"Mama, where are you going?" Rose wondered.

"I'll be back in a few minutes."

As soon as she heard the front door shut, Rose ran into the parlor and looked out one of the windows. Mama was marching up the street toward the schoolhouse, where Miss Sarah would be straightening up and making her lessons for the next day.

Rose went back to the kitchen and began to peel the potatoes. She was so excited she could hardly keep the parings thin. She had peeled only three when she heard the front door open and shut. Mama burst into the kitchen. She jerked out her hatpins, took off her hat, and stabbed the hatpins back into it.

"Mama," Rose began. "Mama, did you . . . tell her?"

"No!" she exclaimed. "She's gone buggy-riding with him, with that Wade Tucker. Buggy-riding! On Monday! At this hour!"

When Papa came home a few minutes later, he said, "That team Wade drives, she'll be lucky if she doesn't come back with a broken neck." He was thoughtful for a moment, pulling at his mustache. "Well, Wade's a clever one. Now he doesn't have any witnesses hiding in the bushes."

Mama clapped the fry pan onto the stove. "She ought to have better sense!" She growled it, as if crying out against some injustice to her own self.

"It's none of our business," Papa said firmly.

"Well, I guess it is," Mama said, digging into the lard pot with a wooden spoon and flinging a dollop into the pan. "She's our boarder, and a good, respectable woman being talked about like that. We have our own situation to think of, too."

"We'll manage," Papa said simply. "I've got to go milk the cow."

Supper that night was painfully quiet. Except for passing the plates, Miss Sarah ate in silence. Her face had an angelic glow, and her lips a hint of a smile. Elsa had been right, Rose realized with a shock. Poor Miss Sarah was gone on Wade Tucker, who was lower than a snake. She fought to control her urge to blurt something foolish.

The next day everyone knew that Jessie Nickles was trying to get out of paying off his bet with Wade Tucker. Wade had told the men at the barbershop that he'd kissed Miss Sarah, but he couldn't prove it. Papa said that at the livery barn one of the men had told Wade, "If you tried handling that team with one hand, you're more of a fool than I gave you credit for."

"Or maybe a better driver," Wade had said, grinning. "Oh, I was driving with one arm, all right!"

Blanche said her father had been talking to the other men on the school board about Miss Sarah.

"They think they ought to take notice of the scandal," Blanche reported. "Not this year, of course. School's out this week, anyway. But they mightn't hire her back for next term."

Rose wanted to cry. "Oh, it's too awful!" she wailed. "But it isn't her fault. Maybe it isn't even true!"

Blanche shrugged. "Papa says a teacher who's talked about isn't setting a right example to the children."

The air of tension at home that week was so thick it made Rose's skin tingle just to be in the house. Then came the last day of school. Two days later, on a gray late-spring Sunday, with the birds chirping their hearts out and the promise of rain in the air, Rose went with Mama, Papa, and the Cooleys to the depot, to see Paul off to Iowa.

He looked so handsome in a boiled collar and Mr. Cooley's best suit, which Mrs. Cooley had altered for him. The jacket was a little loose around the shoulders, but he would soon grow into it. He was as tall as Papa now, and Mrs. Cooley had given him a gold chain to hold Mr. Cooley's railroad watch. No one said it, but Rose felt the empty space of Mr. Cooley. He ought by rights to have been there. He would have been proud.

George hardly spoke as they waited. When the train finally came wheezing into the depot, and they gathered by the door of the passenger car for their last good-byes, he shook Paul's hand stiffly and looked away. First his father had died, and now Paul was going away. At that moment Rose felt sorrier for George than for herself.

Her feelings for Paul had tempered just as his had blossomed for his new work. She was very sorry to see him go, but not so devastated as she had been at New Year's. After Paul had kissed his mother, and shook Mama's and Papa's hands, he turned to Rose.

She put out her hand to shake, but he hesitated a moment, looking deep into her eyes. "Gosh," he said, his voice husky, "I'm gonna miss you something awful, Rose." Then he grabbed her in a tight hug for an instant, and kissed her on the cheek. Her skin burned where his lips had touched.

He held her by the shoulders and looked into her face again. Rose felt her eyes flood with tears.

"Don't you go away anywhere," he said brusquely. "I'll be back. You write now, and I'll write you too. Maybe even send you a wire now and again."

Rose fought to stifle a sob. "I will. I promise."

The conductor called, "All aboard!" Paul picked up his grip and mounted the steps. Mrs. Cooley dabbed a handkerchief to her eyes, and everyone waved.

"Good-bye!" "Take care!" "You be sure and eat right, now!" "I will, don't you worry!" "'Bye!"

The cars banged as the engine lurched forward. Then Paul was gone, in a swirl of bitter coal smoke. Rose stood stock-still, in stunned silence, watching the red lanterns on the last car until they disappeared around the bend. A gust of chill air blew scraps of paper along the tracks, and the first drops of rain spattered on her cheeks.

The Accident

Warm May days had come, and now on Sundays the big girls went walking with their beaux. The younger girls followed them in couples. In their new summer lawns, Rose and Blanche strolled along the railroad tracks, out to the trestle at one end of town and back, then out to the cut at the other end.

Violets and buttercups nodded in the wind along the grade. Peach trees shimmered pink with blossoms, and wild plums let down a flurry of tiny white petals. Rose and Blanche practiced their balance on the rails. If you could walk eleven of them without falling off, you could make a wish that would come true.

From the other end of the railroad cut, the couples left the rails and came back into town along the country road. They passed the graveyard, where old headstones slanted above the graves and the breeze made a mournful sighing in the pines. Then there was the long boardwalk stretching all the way to the square and the end of Sunday afternoon.

The strollers were scattered along the road, ambling in the warm dust, when a racketing clatter made every head whirl. Wade Tucker's black team came charging, running away.

The mad horses seemed gigantic, their great shoulders and steel-shod hooves plunging at Rose and Blanche. Foam flew from their mouths, and dust billowed from their hooves. The girls ran shrieking. One of the big boys dashed toward the horses, to grab at the bridles. But at the last moment he faltered and shrank back.

Rose caught a glimpse of Wade Tucker,

bareheaded, standing off his seat, his feet braced, his weight and strength on the lines, fighting. Miss Sarah, white and still, gripped the edge of the seat.

The air swirled, and then the dust hid them. Rose never saw the crash, but she heard its rending sound. Everyone ran to see. What was left of the buggy lay smashed against a tree, one wheel still spinning crazily. Miss Sarah lay flat on the ground. The big boys, running toward her, paused and swerved aside. Her black cotton stockings could be seen almost to the knees, in a swirl of petticoats.

Before the girls could reach her, she had stirred and was pulling her skirts down. Wade Tucker lay in a crumpled huddle by the tree. The big boys ran over to him and then stood staring at his lifeless body.

Miss Sarah got to her feet. Blood stained her face. The pansy turban hung crooked on her loosened hair. She trembled all over, but she spoke as firmly as she did in school.

"Don't touch him!" she ordered. "You girls

keep back. Oscar, run for the doctor, quick!"

Rose watched in horror as Miss Sarah knelt down by Wade and took hold of his wrist. A strange look came over her face, and her hand jerked away. Then she felt his wrist again, and again let it go.

She kept doing that, while Rose and the rest of the crowd stood, not knowing what to do, not knowing what to say. Rose heard men shouting downtown, heading off Wade's team of horses, which had broken loose.

Young Dr. Hurley, Dr. Padgett's nephew, came hurrying up the long boardwalk carrying his medicine case. Miss Sarah looked up at him. "Get the doctor!" she said.

"I'm a doctor," he told her. He knelt to examine Wade. "My uncle's out on a call."

Men and women were running toward the scene now. A buggy had stopped. Papa came hurrying up, dressed in his Sunday suit, a lit cigar still in his hand.

Miss Sarah's hair had slipped down over her shoulder. One of the big girls took off her crushed turban and began to mop at the blood on her face with a handkerchief. There was only a shallow cut on one pale cheek.

Dr. Hurley stood, slowly shaking his head. Papa asked, "Is he hurt bad, Doc?"

The doctor looked at him, then cast a frowning glance toward Miss Sarah. Papa slowly took off his hat. Then all the other men took off their hats. A woman cried out, "Oh, his poor mother!"

"Is he . . . ?" Miss Sarah began, staring up at the young doctor. "He isn't . . ." She looked around, suddenly seeing all those bare heads. "Oh, no!" she wailed.

"Come, come," Dr. Hurley said, speaking like the old doctor. "Now we don't want you on our hands! We'll do everything that can be done for your husband. Now you just . . ."

Several women gasped, and he looked around in wonderment at the faces.

"He isn't my husband," Miss Sarah said quietly. The doctor turned red. Elsa Beaumont began to laugh. It was horrifying but she couldn't stop herself. Miss Sarah straightened up on her knees.

"But I am engaged to him," she declared, and shouted to Elsa, "So don't you laugh at me! Don't you laugh. . . ." Then she broke down into deep sobs.

Many of the women in town didn't go to church that night, and Rose and her family stayed at home tending to Miss Sarah. Some of Mama's lady friends from the Eastern Star were there as well. Other women were at the Tucker house, sitting with Mrs. Tucker in Wade's bedroom.

Wade had been carried home carefully on a set of bedsprings. He was still breathing, but his neck was broken. Old Doctor Padgett had come and tried to help him. Wade's jaw was broken, too. The doctor set it, and gave him morphine for the pain.

It was only a matter of time, everyone knew. There was no hope. Now people could never again say what they really thought of Wade Tucker. They could speak only good of him.

The Wilders' house was so full of people that Rose sat with Blanche outside in the darkness on the front steps, catching fragments of conversation escaping from the open windows, and scooting out of the way when some caller arrived or left. Every lamp in the house burned with its wick turned high. Long shadows of the people moving about inside played on the earth and bushes.

Miss Sarah was in her bed. Dr. Hurley spoke to Mama at the doorway as he left. "She's a sick woman. It's the shock. She must have her rest."

Rose was in shock too, about the accident and the news that Wade Tucker really had asked Miss Sarah to marry him. And now he lay dying so soon after. It was like something from a book.

"It's so sad," Rose told Blanche. "Widowed before she was even married."

A clutch of the littler boys were hanging over the railing along the street, giggling and knocking each other's hats off.

"Why don't you just go on and mind your business," Rose called out angrily. They grumbled and drifted across to the other side of the street, into the dark shadows, pushing and punching each other.

"They couldn't've been engaged more than an hour or two," Blanche said. "Maybe only some minutes. To think it's all over, so soon."

"Do you think she'll wear mourning for him?" Rose asked.

"Well, she must wear black, of course. But she can't hardly go into widow's weeds. It isn't as if she'd been married to him."

But at least it wasn't Miss Sarah's fault, anymore, that she hadn't been.

The next morning Rose helped Mama nurse Miss Sarah. Her sheets must be changed each day, and her food brought to her in bed.

Young Dr. Hurley called the next morning, and the next. He was very gentle and held Miss Sarah's hand to comfort her. Rose thought he was terribly kind. He had a gaunt, raw-boned, country face, but when he smiled it lighted up pleasantly. He spoke softly to her, trying to pick up her spirits.

Rose lingered near the doorway. Mama

hovered over Miss Sarah on the other side of the bed from Dr. Hurley.

"Your cut is mending well," he told her. "Why, you'll be up and about in no time at all."

But Miss Sarah barely nodded an answer. Her eyes looked without seeing, empty and faraway. She didn't cry, or pout. She just lay there on her pillow, her hair fixed in a bun by Mama, her arms resting along her sides.

Mama cleared her throat. "Perhaps you'll like to dress and go to Wade's bedside," she whispered so softly Rose had to strain to hear over the chiming of the clock. Miss Sarah turned her head away on the pillow.

"You ought to make the effort," Mama urged. "If he's conscious at the last, and you not there, you'll be sorry after he's gone."

"No," Miss Sarah said. "Thank you, I . . . No."

It wasn't like Miss Sarah not to make an effort. She didn't have a broken bone, or even a sprain, but she stayed in bed and hardly talked at all.

When Rose brought her broth or jelly for

her corn bread, Miss Sarah said nothing more than "Thank you." When Mama said how sad it was and how mysterious of providence to take her intended, and they so newly engaged, she said simply, "Yes."

So many of the ladies in town came to call, and Rose didn't like the way some of them tried to wheedle out of Miss Sarah the story of how Wade had proposed.

"My, my, and it all over so soon." Mrs. Murray sighed, leaning over from her chair and peering into Miss Sarah's face. "It must have happened that very afternoon, didn't it? You couldn't've been engaged to him more than an hour or two. Were you?"

"No," Miss Sarah replied.

Later, in the kitchen, Rose was filling the woodbox when she heard Mama saying in low tones to Mrs. Cooley, "You could've knocked me over with a feather."

"I should say so," Mrs. Cooley agreed. "The way Wade was talking and all. But if she says it's so. . . . Anyway I reckon he must have asked her, even if he . . ."

"Yes, even if . . . well," Mama said delicately, "maybe it's all turned out for the best."

Wade Tucker was still living that day, and the next, and the next. And the next. It was impossible that he could last through each night, but in the morning they heard from Dr. Hurley that he had made it to another sunrise. Some of the women were taking turns sitting up with him now.

Miss Sarah stayed in her bed, on Dr. Hurley's orders. He told Mama not to try to get her up, especially to visit Wade. Every morning he said more firmly, "She must get some rest."

The mood around her was sharpening as Wade Tucker clung to life. No one said quite what they were thinking, but there were glances among the callers.

"It's wonderful how he's holding out," Mrs. Beaumont said brightly to Miss Sarah. "It would be providential if he got well. Wouldn't it?" she added with a raised eyebrow.

"Yes," Miss Sarah said weakly. Then she

perked up. "Yes, of course! I hope he does."

Mama piped up, bristling, "Well, of course you do!"

She groused to Mrs. Cooley after, "That Mrs. Beaumont! I'd like to wring her neck!"

Mrs. Cooley sat up with Wade that night. The next morning she came hurrying in while Rose and Mama were doing the breakfast dishes. Mama took her hands out of the dishwater at once and began to dry them. "When did he go?" she asked gravely.

"No," Mrs. Cooley breathed excitedly. "No, but . . ." She pulled the door to the dining room closed behind her, shooed Mama into the bedroom, and closed that door too. Rose crept across the kitchen and put her ear to the keyhole.

"Oh, poor Miss Sarah," Mrs. Cooley's muffled voice was saying. "And his mother. Mrs. Tucker said right out that Miss Sarah was a liar. She said, 'It's a bare-faced lie!' Those very words. 'My poor boy never thought for one minute to marry that old maid.' "

Rose heard Mama gasp. Then she said indignantly, "Everybody knows Miss Sarah's never told a lie in her life. If she says they were engaged, then they *were* engaged. And I don't know what good it'll do Mrs. Tucker to—"

"But that's not all!"

Old Dr. Padgett had seen Wade that morning and said, miracle of miracles, that he seemed to be mending. He'd seen men survive worse things than a broken neck. It all depended on if his spinal cord was injured. But the old doctor had said he wouldn't be the least surprised to have him up and about as good as new one of these days.

Rose leaned against the wall wide-eyed, barely breathing.

"It's all that young doctor's doing," Mrs. Cooley said. "If only he hadn't jumped to conclusions and said Wade was her husband. Poor Miss Sarah. It'll be all over town."

The creak of a floorboard startled Rose. She nearly tripped over the woodbox sprinting across the kitchen. She snatched a rag and started wiping the table just as the bedroom door opened. Mama came out looking grim and harried.

A Good Ending

All over Mansfield there were dirty dishes and unmade beds. The news that Mrs. Tucker had said Wade never would marry Miss Sarah, and that he might live to walk and talk again, had set the town humming with gossip.

Miss Sarah's room was crowded with callers, and there were more people outside by the porch. In the kitchen Mama was telling Mrs. Helfinstine, "Well, that's very kind of you. Crabapple, too! I was saying to Miss Sarah, 'What will you ever do with all this jelly?' "

On the porch Mrs. Loftin murmured on her way out, "She looks like death. And no wonder."

But looking in at her from the doorway of her bedroom, Rose didn't think Miss Sarah looked like death. She was sitting up in bed, in her snow-white nightgown with a tucked and lace-edged collar buttoned to her chin. Her face was so thin that her cheeks were faintly hollowed.

The tawny braids of her hair hung straight down over either shoulder, and her eyes looked enormous. Her thin cheeks, the firm curves of her pale lips, and her heavy-lidded eyes gave Rose a strange sensation. She knew Miss Sarah was old, and no one said she was pretty. But Rose could not stop gazing at her.

Miss Sarah had said it was time she got up. Mama was fussing over her. "No, Miss Sarah. You stay right where you are until the doctor comes."

Mrs. Beaumont pushed past Rose into the room. "I don't know's there's so much the matter with her," she said. "Seems to me she might as well get up now as later."

Lois, her oldest daughter, who had ruined her own reputation two years before with a boy from Seymour, had come with her. She stood in the corner by the washstand.

"Yes," she blurted out in a haughty voice. "Either she's engaged to him or she isn't, and I guess he knows. Hiding here in bed won't make any difference."

Rose flinched at her words. A jolt of electricity ran through the room. Everyone looked at Miss Sarah. A thin flush ran up her cheeks, and her lips parted. But Mama spoke first. She looked like a mule ready to kick.

"That's enough from you, miss!" she said to Lois. "Children should be seen and not heard." She had made an enemy of Mrs. Beaumont, but she didn't care.

Mrs. Beaumont gave Mama a hard look, and turned to Miss Sarah. "You are engaged to him," she said smoothly. "Aren't you?"

"It's disgraceful, " Mrs. Cooley exclaimed. "You leave her alone, the doctor says she's sick. . . ."

Then Miss Sarah finally spoke. She said,

firmly, "I certainly am engaged to him."

Everyone was staggered. Mrs. Beaumont gasped, "Why, but he's getting well!"

Rose watched in thrall as Miss Sarah pulled herself up and leaned forward, her head wavering ever so slightly like a snake ready to strike. Her hands clenched the counterpane spread, and her eyes flashed angrily.

"I'm glad he's getting better. I hope he gets well. I'd never have let the whole town know what's only our business, if I'd been myself at the time. I wish him well, only I've changed my mind since. I've had time to think it over. And if I want to break my engagement, I don't see it's any of your business."

Mrs. Beaumont gasped, but there was nothing for her to say. She was beaten at her own pettiness.

Rose thought Miss Sarah was wonderful.

"And now I'll be obliged to you," Miss Sarah said calmly, "if you'll all step out for a minute, so I can get up and dress."

But she didn't get up right away. Dr. Hurley was already at the gate, and there was barely time to hide her nightgown under a dressing sacque.

The young doctor wasn't used to being a doctor yet. He tried to act like Dr. Padgett, but he was nervous with so many women watching him. He gripped his medicine case and was awkward about lifting his hat. Someone near the gate asked him, "How is he, Doctor?"

"He's improving," Dr. Hurley answered. "He's conscious and taking nourishment."

"Oh, Doctor." Mrs. Beaumont pounced like a cat. "Has he talked yet? What did he say?"

"He can't speak," he told her. "His jaw's broken. And we are keeping him perfectly quiet. Nobody can see him." He repeated, "Nobody."

When he had gone, stiff-backed, into Miss Sarah's room, Mrs. Beaumont snorted, "Well!" Her husband owned the bank. She wasn't used to being spoken to like that. And the idea of keeping people out of Wade's room, when he was sick! "The very idea!" she said.

Mama and Mrs. Cooley came out of Miss Sarah's room with Dr. Hurley. They walked him to the door and came back into the kitchen. "And I for one believe every word of it," Mama was saying.

"Miss Sarah wouldn't lie, for a fact," Mrs. Cooley said. "She couldn't do such a thing to save her life. And besides, it serves Wade Tucker right!"

Mama closed the kitchen door, checked to see if anyone was standing outside the backdoor, and asked Mrs. Cooley, "How old is he?"

"Twenty-nine last February," Mrs. Cooley said.

"Well, that's a good three years."

"Yes," Mrs. Cooley said, nodding. "I thought you'd noticed. You think she did?"

"No, not yet," Mama replied. "She's had too much else on her mind. Goodness, it seems almost too much to hope for, with all the girls setting their caps for him the way they have."

Rose understood nothing of what they were saying, but suddenly Mama caught her listening and remembered the wash to be taken in from the line.

One Sunday afternoon soon after, Rose and Mama and Papa were sitting on the front porch after dinner. A buggy passed by carrying Miss Sarah, with the young doctor at the reins. Rose stared in astonishment.

Miss Sarah wore her cashmere and an old hat. She sat stiffly, knowing everyone was watching. Dr. Hurley stared straight ahead, driving the gentle livery-stable team as if it took all his attention. The buggy went up the street, past the schoolhouse, and out of town, where the apple orchards were in full blossom.

"That young man's got nerve," Papa said, pulling on his pipe. "The way you women-folks gossip in this town, I'd as soon face a den of lions as walk right up in the face and eyes of everybody and start sparking Miss Sarah."

"She's the salt of the earth," Mama said. "And thank goodness one man's got the sense to realize it."

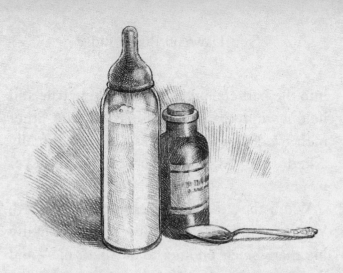

A Mother Never Forgets

Miss Sarah's name soon faded from everyone's lips. People got so used to seeing her out walking with Dr. Hurley on a warm night, or seeing them sitting together at a debate, that folks thought of them as good as married. Of course, Miss Sarah said it would be only proper to wait a spell before the wedding.

"We think next spring would be a pleasant time," she said one night at supper.

Rose thought it was just wonderful the way things had turned out. When he was well enough to walk about, Wade Tucker had crept into the barbershop one day, looking pale and holding himself stiffly. Papa said the other men tried to get him to say if he had really asked Miss Sarah to marry, but he never would.

When they teased him about being jilted, Wade would only say, "There's no woman living that's smart enough to outsmart me—and don't you think she did it!"

Soon after, on a blistering hot summer day, Miss Sarah moved out of the Wilders' house. She went to live with Dr. Hurley's uncle and aunt, Dr. and Mrs. Padgett. She would help Dr. Padgett in his office, until school took up again in the fall. It was a good arrangement for her, Mama said.

"And just as well for us, because we have the farm to take care of. With the corn needing to be hoed, and the hay ready to cut, we'll be too busy to have any boarders until after we pick our first crop of apples."

"Maybe we won't even need boarders again," Papa said, grinning. "We had a mild spring with no late frost, and plenty of rain.

The apples set up jim dandy. With a little more rain, and then a couple of cool nights come August—why, by Christmas we could just be sitting on an easy street."

"There never was an easy street that wasn't hard to find," Mama joked with a crooked smile.

In July, Abe and Effie had another baby, a big boy they named Earl. He looked so pink and healthy. The twins, James and Elza, couldn't stop fussing over him. It thrilled Rose to have another little one on the farm to sew for and tickle and spoil.

But after a week Earl wasn't keeping down his milk. He grew weaker and weaker. As hungry as he must have been, the poor thing seemed to have hardly any appetite.

Mama and Abe begged Effie to let Dr. Padgett or Dr. Hurley come out and look after him. But Effie wouldn't hear of it. "He's just a mite colicky, I reckon. James and Elza was the same when they was babies."

She sat on the porch of the farmhouse with

Earl in her arms, shooing flies and rocking gently. She tried to get little Earl to suck his milk from a new manufactured thing that Mama had gotten from a catalogue. It was a rubber nipple you could snap onto a bottle of milk. Mama thought maybe Earl would drink sweetened cow's milk.

Rose watched from the kitchen doorway, with a freshly scalded milk jug in her hand. She was going out to the barn to milk Bunting, the Jersey cow. They had brought her from town for the summer, so she could graze on good pasture and Effie would have enough milk.

Effie put the nipple to Earl's tiny mouth. "C'mon now," she whispered. "Ain't you hungry? Sure you is."

But Earl's mouth puckered, and his face squinched. Then he turned his head away. When Effie chased his mouth with the nipple, his tiny hands waved helplessly, trying to push it away. He cried out in a faint mewl that broke Rose's heart. Effie sighed heavily and bit her lip.

Mama sat at Effie's feet, on the steps, peeling potatoes. Abe hovered over Effie's chair, his fists jammed in the pockets of his tattered overalls. He stared hard at the baby in Effie's arms, as if he could will him to suck. Some crows flew past nearby, their raucous calls echoing across the barnyard.

"You can't be too careful," Mama said, her brow furrowed. "You never can tell, and Dr. Padgett is a fine doctor. He keeps up with all the latest scientific advancements."

"We ain't got no five dollars cash money for no doctor," Effie blurted. There was an edge in her voice.

Mama bent to her potatoes, silent for a long moment. The only sound came from Abe's boots pacing on the porch like a ticking clock. Then Mama said, slowly, "Perhaps Mr. Wilder and I, we could find some arrangement. Something through the church, perhaps. We might be able—"

"Well now, that's downright—" Abe began.

Effie interrupted him, her voice firm and proud. "I thank you kindly, Mrs. Wilder. But you already done a heap of kindness for us as it is. I reckon we can manage it somehow. I got my folks to help, and the granny woman. Leastways, we Stubbinses are from strong stock. Earl's a-going to be just fine."

Then Effie tried to give poor little Earl a spoonful of Dr. Boschee's Infant Soothing Syrup, a patent medicine. Since the day Earl was born, she'd kept a bottle of it, with its bright-yellow label, by her side. Effie's mother, Mrs. Stubbins, had given it to Effie when she was a baby.

A little of the syrup went in his mouth, but most of it spilled down his chin.

Mama shot Rose a worried glance.

Almost everyone they knew used patent medicines. Hardly a cupboard in town didn't have a bottle of Lydia Pinkham's Remedy for Women hidden there, or Burdock's Blood Bitters, or Doctor Pierce's Favorite Prescription, or Colden's Liquid Beef Tonic.

Nearly every magazine printed advertisements for those medicines. The advertisements said the medicines would cure everything bad that could ever happen to a person, even make the lame to walk and the blind to see.

The people who made some of those medicines also gave away almanacs to the farmers, with places to check the phases of the moon, and to write in the weather and planting dates. The almanacs were packed with letters from satisfied customers who had been cured. There were articles bragging about the medicines, and cartoons that seemed to Rose a bit naughty. She found one that showed how a woman had increased her bustline by stuffing her dress with cotton batting. Rose saw that cartoon when she was by herself, and still she blushed.

"Do not think your lungs are in perfect condition because your physician said so," she had read in an almanac advertisement for Green's Great Dyspeptic Panacea.

Some of the medicine companies sent wagons around the countryside to visit town squares and drum up business. Rose and Mama had seen the Hamlin's Wizard Oil

show when it came to Mansfield the year
before.

Hamlin's wagon was a fancy four-seater
open coach with a fringed roof. The wagon
was painted bright red with yellow and blue
trim, pulled by a team of four perfectly
matched mares. Painted in fancy gold letters
on both sides of the wagon box were the
words HAMLIN'S WIZARD OIL. The wagon
had a four-man band sitting in it that played
humorous and sentimental songs.

Between songs a fifth man in a morning
coat stood in the back of the wagon, holding
up a bottle, and bellowing to the crowd:

"Folks wanna know, How can Wizard Oil
work? Why, it's just too good to be true, they
say. Well, I'll let you good people in on a little
secret," he said, leaning toward the crowd.
"Wizard Oil acts directly upon the nervous
system. It allays pain almost instantly by
virtue of its sedative properties.

"But don't you take my word on it. No sirree. Just ask the folks from coast to coast,

millions of 'em, who'll tell you straight out that our product has performed radical and permanent cures for man's every known affliction.

"Just a mere four bits, ladies and gents," he said, waving his derby. "Is four bits too much to pay to cure the rheumatism in six days, guaranteed or your money back? We stand by our product," he promised. "Neuralgia pains gone in ten minutes! Diphtheria in twelve hours! What're you folks waiting for? Step right up!

"Boys, how about another tune for the nice folks? Somethin' stimulating."

The band struck up a lively tune as farmers in overalls mingled with the town folks crowding around the wagon, eagerly searching their pockets for fifty cents for a small bottle, a dollar for the big size.

"Oh, that's just so much *claptrap*!" Mama sputtered. Some nearby heads turned, and people stared at her. Both Mama and Papa had been struck down by diphtheria years ago, when Rose was very young. They were deathly sick for weeks and weeks.

Mama said no such potion could have cured them in half a day. "If it hadn't been for the doctor, we'd neither of us have gotten our health back."

The *Ladies Home Journal* had printed articles warning about patent medicines. The writer said they were frauds made up from nothing more than liquor and sleeping powders.

Miss Sarah had told them at dinner one day how worried Dr. Hurley was about folks thinking patent medicines could fix their ailments. He said people had died from believing it.

"It's a downright crime what these big businessmen will do to put a dollar in their pockets," Miss Sarah had said.

It wasn't until little Earl was deathly sick that Effie finally changed her mind. Nate came galloping into town one morning on Nellie, one of the mules. Both Dr. Padgett and Dr. Hurley were out on calls. When Dr. Hurley finally reached Rocky Ridge Farm, it was too late.

Rose had had only a few hard cries in her life. This was another. She helped Mama and Mrs. Stubbins clean the farmhouse and cook while Granny Albers, the old yarbwoman, came to lay out the baby's body.

She made a bed for him out of a bushel apple box. She lined it with muslin and a layer of white sateen. She dressed the baby in a white gown and tied on a white bonnet edged with lace. She made up a blush of berries to pink up his cheeks and rouge his tiny lips.

Then she set the bed on the porch, propped on a chair, for the mourners to see when they came. Mama placed a small bouquet of daisies next to him in the little box. The grown-up women took turns sitting with the baby, shooing away flies with a turkey feather.

Effie stayed in her bed. Abe disappeared for a long time. Then the sounds of sawing and hammering coming from the barn told of his building Earl's coffin. The twins had been sent to the Stubbins farm, with Nate to watch over them.

Mr. Stubbins paid for a man to come out to the farm and make a photograph of Earl in his little bed. That way Abe and Effie would always be able to remember what he looked like.

The baby looked exactly as if he were peacefully asleep, like a doll in its crib, as if he would wake any moment and cry to be fed. When Rose looked at him, she could not hold back her tears any longer. Mama held her a long while in the kitchen, until her sobs faded to hiccups.

Rose knew that babies sometimes died. There were often stories in the *Mansfield Mail* telling of babies who died of yellow fever, or children who choked to death on watermelon seeds, or got trampled by a horse.

She knew God had a special place in his heart whenever he took an innocent to his bosom. But she couldn't help feeling angry with Effie for being so stubborn. She couldn't help despairing that a tender life should end before it had a chance to begin.

Earl was buried in the graveyard of Wolf Creek Church, at the end of a weedy set of wagon tracks in the forest. "The Lord giveth and the Lord taketh away," the preacher said. As Rose listened she remembered the time she tried to save a nest full of baby birds that had been knocked out of a tree by a storm. She couldn't find anything they would eat, and one by one they had weakened and died.

Rose wept silently when it was her turn to throw a handful of earth into the grave.

Mama had held herself strong throughout, grim and quiet and busy with the extra chores. But when they came home from the burial, after she'd taken off her gloves and unpinned her hat, she sat down at the kitchen table and buried her head in her hands. Then, for the first time Rose had ever heard, Mama sobbed her heart out.

That brought a fresh flood of grief from Rose. Even Papa could not stop himself from shedding noiseless tears. They sat around the table, red-eyed and weepy, trying to gather themselves up again. Finally Mama mopped her face with her handkerchief. She took Papa's hand in one of hers, and Rose's in the other. Rose could feel the calluses on her hot, dry palm.

"I'm sorry," Mama said. "It's just I can't help remembering our own little boy."

Papa nodded, snuffling. "I been thinking of it myself."

"When the preacher said Earl's name, it . . . it just tore at me that we never did give that child his own name before we buried him," she said mournfully.

Rose was stunned. She had forgotten all about her baby brother who had died all those years before in South Dakota. He had been just a week or so old. He had died suddenly when Rose was very little, too young to understand, or to remember for herself.

"Oh, Mama," Rose cried out, fresh tears wetting her cheeks. "I'm so sorry."

Mama sighed heavily, gazing at Rose's hand

and caressing it. Softly she said, "A mother never forgets, Rose. I might not speak of it, but as surely as you have been by my side, he has always been in my heart. When a mother loses a child, she never forgets."

First Harvest

Dear Paul,
It seems that you have been away such a
terribly long time. There is so much news to
tell. Your letter was very good to get. We all
sat in the parlor, and Mama read it to us.
It is very sad that you cannot come home
this year. We will miss you for Christmas
most of all.

Rose sat at the kitchen table one Sunday
afternoon with a sheet of Mama's writing
paper. Mama and Papa had driven out to the
farm to look over the orchard. Rose paused,

chewing the end of her pencil, listening to the fading whistle of an express train that had just passed by the back of the house, heading west.

She could hear a wagon rattle past on the street, and a screen door slap shut at the Gaskills'. A lone mockingbird warbled its ever-changing song from the maple tree in the backyard. Many of the spring birds had finished raising their young and had ceased their singing. Soon the wrens would be flying south. The damp, oveny air quivered with the rasping of grasshoppers and cicadas.

The sweetness of summer seemed to grow more urgent as it neared an end. It was already the last of July, and Rose felt a yearning to hold back the season. Spring always came on so slowly, and summer departed in such haste.

Rose wrote Paul about Miss Sarah, and about Earl.

I think it is very hard to live a life that is truly joyful. I do so want to, but always there is a new sorrow or hard times to steal away the happiness. Mrs. Rippee says life is an onion that you peel crying, and only fools live a merry life. If that is true, anyone should want to be born a fool!

Just now I am lonely. Blanche is away. Mr. Coday took the family to Chicago and Niagara Falls. How I would like to see the Falls!

I hope you are finding Grinnell to your liking. Everyone misses you very much. So many people have asked after you!

What do you think of President McKinley? Everyone in town thinks he is a bully for the wealthy interests and the trusts. The newspapers have the most cruel cartoons of him, and some men even write that he should be killed. It's horrible the way people talk! They say he is the most hated creature on the American continent. But Papa thinks Mr. Bryan hasn't a chance in the world to beat him in the election.

Do you think it is wrong for a girl to wonder about such things? After all, we

cannot vote in Missouri, or hardly any-
where. But I cannot help myself. I think
about what the future will bring for us.

Some weeks later, Papa brought home from
the post office a letter Paul had written just to
Rose. She took it up to her attic room and
greedily ripped it open.

Dear Friend Rose,
*   I think also for the future, and I am lonely*
here as well. Grinnell is a good enough town,
with an opera house and a butcher. There are
miles of cornfields all 'round, far as the eye
can see. The town folks are friendly, and the
depot master has me to his house for Sunday
dinners.
*   But I miss home and Mother and George*
very much, and your family as well, of course.
I might be sent on a different assignment
for this winter. The dispatcher says they will
have need of an operator in Cairo, Illinois,
and I am getting fast enough on the key to
work in a bigger town with more train

*orders. It would bring an increase in my
pay, too.*

   Maybe in between I can make a visit home.
   *No, I do not think there is anything
shameful about a girl who thinks about
things. You were always smart in school, and
why shouldn't girls have the vote anywhere
they like? Maybe someday they will. Women
vote in four states already.*

Rose's heart leaped with joy to read that
Paul was also lonely. It was a feeling for them
to share. Even if she could not see him, she
could imagine Paul late at night, bent over
the clattering telegraph key in an empty
depot in a strange town, missing home. There
was a wicked comfort in that. She didn't really
want Paul to be unhappy. She just wanted
him to miss *her*.

As the summer wore on, the anchor of conversation around the dining table was the
weather and the coming apple harvest. Papa
and Mama might trade some small gossip

about the folks in town, or how Effie was holding up, or conditions in the country.

Theodore Roosevelt, the governor of New York, had been picked to be Mr. McKinley's new vice president, if he won the election in November for a second term. President McKinley was fat and lazy, the newspapers said. Mr. Roosevelt had fought against the Spanish in Cuba and was an outdoorsman. He was such a rousing speech-maker that his words started a riot in Colorado.

"They ought to make Roosevelt the president, and McKinley the vice president," Papa said. "That McKinley's got about as much heart as a possum. What this country needs is a tiger."

But always Mama and Papa turned their thoughts again to the orchard, like bees hurrying home to the hive. For six years, since they first bought the farm, they had worried about those trees. The orchard was their future. The hay, the oats, the corn, the garden, the timber—these things could feed them and the livestock almost all year, and provide Abe and Effie with their shares to live on as well. But all the potatoes and railroad cross ties they could take off the farm would never get them ahead.

A few good apple harvests could bring in enough cash money to pay off the mortgage. Then they wouldn't have any more debt. They would be beholden to no one. They would be free.

Mama and Papa hated debt the way horses hate snakes. "Even if he has nothing, a body who owes nothing is rich," Mama liked to say. "Remember that, Rose."

The first winter they had to chase wild hogs that had been eating the bark off the young saplings. They had to build a long fence around the whole twenty acres of orchard. Papa and Abe split every rail and post themselves. After a terrible ice storm they froze their fingers knocking the ice from the branches so they wouldn't split and crack.

They had whitewashed the trunks each spring to keep the sun from burning the bark.

Papa put up a bee gum. The bees helped pollinate the blossoms so the trees could produce better fruit.

Each year some trees had been lost or were in danger from one calamity or another. Wood borers killed a few. They had watched helplessly when a killing drought stunted the trees' growth. A tornado destroyed almost a quarter of them, and once a forest fire nearly burned up the whole orchard.

But most of the trees survived, through providence and hard work. Papa had studied books about fruit orchards, and had talked to other orchard men in the county. He could go on for hours about how much extra wood growth could be cut each year without hurting the tree. He spoke of shaping the trees, cutting crossed branches and water sprouts and dead wood.

When Rose would stroll through the orchard with Papa, his eyes did not wander over the whole hillside as Rose's did. He would study one tree at a time, reading the hidden meaning in the leaves, the twigs, and the bark, like paragraphs in a book.

He would come home from a trip to Hartville, the county seat, full of gossip about different kinds of apples. The Jonathan ripened early, but its stems dried out quickly, and a bad storm could turn a whole crop into falls that were hardly worth the trouble to pick them up. The York Imperial couldn't be beat for heavy bearing and it was a fine cooker, too, but an orchard man could count on a good crop but once every two years. Arkansas blacks were good keepers. They lasted all winter and stayed sweet. But they turned a very deep red when ripe. The market wanted brighter color.

The Wilders' trees were Ben Davises. It was a popular kind of apple to grow in the Ozarks, but it ripened late, so it was harder to get to market when the price for apples was high.

If Rose had heard Papa talk once about the weather, she had heard it a thousand times: the effect of cool or warm spring weather on the buds, the bloom, the set, and the harvest.

What the best weather was against the coddling moths that laid the eggs that hatched into the worms that would eat the apples before they could be picked. Fungus disease, leafhoppers, the effects of rain or lack of rain, too much sunshine and not enough—Papa knew it all.

He had shoveled countless wagonloads of manure on the ground to feed the trees. He hauled more wagonloads of wood ash to put around the trunks. The ashes sweetened the earth and kept away wood borers and diseases.

He had planted cover crops between the trees, to hold the moisture in the soil and keep the earth from washing away.

For six years the orchard had been the dream that pulled them through the dark hours. When the orchard came into bearing, they would have everything they wanted. Now, finally, the first crop hung heavy and green on the trees, waiting for the right weather to color the apples up for market.

This year the weather had been perfect—

just enough rain to keep the fruit growing, just enough sunshine to bring out the color. After an early cool spell in the beginning of September, the apples showed the first blush of pink.

All summer Papa had been hauling wagon-loads of empty barrels to the farm, buying them when he could find them for a low price. Now he set them out in the orchard, more than two hundred, lined up in rows like soldiers marching to battle.

He and Abe hammered together extra ladders made from the trunks of small cedar trees. Papa fixed it with the Stubbinses and two other families who would help pick in exchange for a share of the crop. Mr. Stubbins had had his own orchard, but the fire started by sparks from a passing train two years before burned most of them up. It would be a long while before his new trees were ready to bear.

At harvest time, the telegraph operators at the depot posted the latest prices for all the crops on a blackboard outside the telegraph office. Each day Papa reported the price at which apples were shipping. When the first apples began to go to market from orchards farther south, and from orchards of early-bearing varieties, Papa came into the house one evening with a spring in his step.

"Bess, the market's at two dollars four bits a barrel!" he crowed. "Gosh, if only we had something to ship! We must have a hundred fifty barrels out there if we've got a single bushel. Think of it, Bess! Three hundred seventy-five dollars, just sitting there waiting to be had!"

We Aren't Rich Yet

Finally the day came when the tops of the trees showed bright red, and Papa said the picking could begin the next morning. It dawned drizzly and raw, but Papa said nothing would stop them from getting those apples off the trees.

"The market's already dropped two bits. I hear they're just a week off from picking in Illinois. When those crops come to market, the price is sure to fall. There's not a day to lose."

Abe, Papa, Nate, and George Cooley worked with the pickers, carrying buckets up the ladders into the top branches. Papa told

Rose and Mama to keep an eye on the younger pickers.

"I was a boy myself," he said. "I guess I know how many apples a little shaver can stuff in his stomach in a day's time. And we don't want good apples spoiled by throwing fights, either."

Mama and Rose worked with Mr. and Mrs. Stubbins and Mrs. Cooley at the culler, which was set at the edge of the orchard. The culler was a table in the shape of a triangle. It had a little wall around all the sides and a slatted bottom. It sat up on legs that tilted the table toward the pointed end. The baskets of apples were gently dumped in the wide side, and as they rolled toward the point, the dead leaves and stems fell through the open spaces between the slats to the ground.

It was Rose's job to lift up the heavy baskets, dump the apples onto the table, and keep pushing them down toward the point.

Mama, Mrs. Stubbins, and Mrs. Cooley stood alongside the culler picking out the imperfect apples—the ones with scale marks, or worm holes, or bruises—and packing them into barrels. Those apples would sell for little money, and they would be used for making cider or apple butter or for drying. Whoever bought them would make them into something right away, because bruised and imperfect apples spoiled quickly.

The apples that made it all the way to the point of the culling table were the good apples that they hoped to sell at market prices. Mr. Stubbins packed them into a barrel by himself, because he had done it so many times before.

He kept two barrels going. One was for number one grade, which must be at least two and one half inches in diameter. The other he packed with number two grade apples, which were smaller and might have a few blemishes.

Mr. Stubbins hands flew as he worked. He looked at every apple, checking for bruises and flaws. No bruised apple should find its way into the number ones and number twos. By the time those barrels might be opened in some far-off city, maybe not until next spring, one rotten apple could have spoiled a whole barrel of perfect number ones.

If the apples were a bit too wet, Mr. Stubbins dried them with a rag. Too much moisture in a barrel could turn the apples moldy.

As he worked, Mr. Stubbins explained what he was doing, so Mama would learn for herself.

"You want to keep a full basket a-going of the reddest and the best," he explained. "Them'll be for the ring-faces."

"What's a ring-face?" Rose wanted to know. The sun peeked out from a hole in the clouds. She was glad to feel the warmth on her shoulders for a few moments.

"That's the top two rows of the barrel," Mr. Stubbins said, tasting an apple. "These here are just sweet enough. They ought to bring a good price, if the market keeps."

"Is it quite honest?" Mama asked. "To put the good ones on top?"

"There's tricks to ever' trade," Mr. Stubbins answered, his voice hollow-sounding as he leaned into the bottom of the barrel to arrange the ring-face apples. He set them stem-side down in a perfect circle with no spaces between. He had put down a layer of straw first, then the ring-face. When the barrel was full and closed, he would turn it over, and the bottom would become the top. The ring-face would be the first apples the buyer would see.

"It's reckoned thataway by the folks that buys 'em. It all evens up in the end. They get a big price for the best, and a smaller price for the others. It all evens up."

Rose could see the worry lines form on Mama's forehead as she went back to her culling. Mama didn't like to do a thing that was even the tiniest bit deceitful. But Mr. Stubbins had been selling apples a long time from his own orchard. She wouldn't think of disagreeing with him.

Everyone worked hard and steadily. Every few minutes one of the pickers brought a bushel basket full of freshly picked apples. The stooping made Rose's back ache. The constant pushing tortured her shoulders.

The three women stood culling out the apples with knots and rots, and the ones that were too green. Mr. Stubbins did the packing of the best apples into the barrels. After the ring-face had been packed, he filled a bucket with apples, lowered the bucket into the barrel, and tenderly rolled the apples out. As he packed, he shook the barrel now and then, so the fruit would settle properly.

When the barrel was nearly full, he put in another ring-face and another layer of clean straw, and then he hammered in the lid with a wooden mallet. Then he tipped the barrel over and turned it bottom side up.

He took a round stencil made from a piece of cow leather, laid it on the lid, and painted over it with an old brush wet with black paint. When he lifted the stencil off, the top of that barrel had a sign on it that read:

**BEN DAVIS NO. 1
ROCKY RIDGE FARM
MANSFIELD, MISSOURI**

Rose had to stop pushing to go and look, and then so did Mama.

"Oh, my," Mama said happily. "It gives me such a cozy feeling to see our name on there."

Rose's heart was bursting. That was one barrel of their own apples to sell. It had taken a long time to grow them, six years, and a lot of work and worry to fill that barrel. Soon a merchant in St. Louis or Memphis or maybe even Chicago would read that lid when he went to pry it open. He would taste one of the apples, enjoying the satisfying fresh crunch and the winey sweetness on his tongue. He would know that Mama and Papa were proud enough of their apples to put the name of their farm on them. Thinking of it sent a thrill along all of Rose's nerves.

"These here apples are a-coming in mighty green," Mr. Stubbins said as he rolled a fresh empty barrel into place next to the culling table. "A fella likes to clean out the tops of them trees when he's up there. But you oughta tell 'em, Mrs. Wilder, to leave them green ones on to color up proper. Best way to pick an orchard is to do it twice."

So Mama hurried off to scold the pickers not to waste perfectly good apples picking them too soon.

That afternoon, after a cold dinner eaten under the trees, a big empty freight wagon pulled by a team of four horses drove up the hill from Fry Creek.

On the seat sat a tall man with a long handlebar mustache. He wore a wide-brimmed hat and a dark-green duster. He hitched the team to the fence and walked up the hillside to the culler, his sober eyes scanning the trees, wisps of cigar smoke trailing behind. His duster billowed out behind him, showing a pair of tooled boots with silver toes.

"You got your first buyer, Mrs. Wilder," Mr. Stubbins muttered under his breath. "And he looks a sharper, too. 'Member what I told you. Don't be too quick to jump on his price. You got to work 'em up some."

Mama patted her hair and smoothed her

apron. The buyer walked right up to Mr. Stubbins. Without so much as a hello he said gruffly, "You in charge here?"

Mr. Stubbins shook his head as Mama cleared her throat. "I am Mrs. Wilder," she said politely, stepping forward. Rose stopped in the middle of pushing apples to hear. "Mr. Wilder and I own this orchard. How may I help you?"

"Where can I find your husband?" he said, staring over her head into the trees. He towered over Mama's short body.

"My husband is picking," Mama said evenly. Rose saw her back stiffen, the way it always did when she was getting her dander up. "Are you in the market for apples?"

"I ain't lookin' for a haircut and a shave," the buyer sneered. Mama's head snapped as if she'd been slapped. The air around the table crackled. Everyone stopped what they were doing. Mama bit her lip.

The buyer spit a bit of cigar tobacco off his tongue. Then he picked an apple out of the barrel Mr. Stubbins had been packing, pulled out a knife, and sliced it in half. He looked at the seeds for a moment and sniffed the fruit.

"Apples is a man's game," the buyer said, flicking an ash from his cigar. Then he threw the apple halves on the ground, without even taking a bite, and wiped his hands on his kerchief.

Mr. Stubbins frowned, and Rose heard his false upper teeth click. The buyer stared down at him for an instant, and blinked owlishly. Then to Mama he said, "I reckon your husband wouldn't like it much if his wife—"

Mama couldn't hold her tongue a moment longer. "I'll thank you to keep your smart remarks to yourself," she said sharply, planting her fists on her hips. Rose watched transfixed as the buyer flinched. His eyes narrowed, and he looked down at Mama as if he noticed her for the first time. The color flared up Mama's neck, and a red flag of rage flew on her cheeks. He took a step back.

"I don't know where you come from," Mama said in her steeliest voice, her eyes

165

flashing. "But here in the Ozarks we still fancy a civil greeting when we meet a stranger. As for my husband, I told you, he is busy with the picking. If you don't care to make your trade with a woman, perhaps you ought to look in someone else's orchard for the apples you require."

The buyer stirred restlessly. His eyes darted about, as if he were looking for a place to hide.

"Well," he finally said, flashing a thin smile. "I guess these apples're good as any. Course, the market's down quite a bit since yesterday. For what I can see, you've got commercial grade mostly, cannery fruit. The market for fresh apples wants color, and there's more commercial grade apples around than fleas on a yellow cur."

Mama's shoulders sagged a moment. Then she gathered a handful of her skirt, turned and said over her shoulder, "You follow me, Mr. . . ."

"Endicott, of Endicott Packing House, Springfield."

"You follow me, Mr. Endicott. We have all

the color you can take." Then she marched into the orchard, one arm swinging and the other hand holding her hem up. Mr. Endicott loped along after her.

As soon as they were out of earshot, Mr. Stubbins growled, "Dirty, rotten, smart-alecky—"

"Emmett!" Mrs. Stubbins scolded. "Mind your tongue!"

Mr. Stubbins grumbled and bent to his work again. His uppers clicked a few times.

"The nerve of that man," Mrs. Cooley whispered. "Are they all so unpleasant?"

"Like I said afore," Mr. Stubbins said, "There's tricks to ever' trade. These packers, they got a game a-going to make the orchard folks to think their apples ain't no good for number ones. They get me so stirred up, I could chew nails. They can take their durned game and go—"

"*Emmett Stubbins!*" Mrs. Stubbins cried out, scowling hard at him.

Mr. Stubbins sighed. "Well, leastways Mrs. Wilder put him in his place. I got to admire her for that. Never fool with a woman, I always say."

"Never try to *fool* a woman," Mrs. Stubbins corrected him.

Rose admired Mama, too. Mama had a way of showing her temper just so much, and she always seemed to know just what to say when she needed to put a person in his or her place. Rose wished she were so clever. She had learned to hold her tongue most of the time, but she could not keep herself as calm as Mama when she was upset.

The wait for Mama to finish with Mr. Endicott was agony. Every so often Rose caught a glimpse of the two through the trees. They strolled slowly through the orchard as if on a Sunday outing. When Mr. Endicott lifted a branch to look at the fruit, Mama folded her arms and, catlike, looked away with indifference.

Rose knew Mama was anything but indifferent. Would he buy? How much would he buy, and how much would he pay? The suspense was unbearable.

Finally, after a long while, Mama appeared again with Mr. Endicott at the end of a row. She walked him to his wagon and shook his hand, and he drove off. Rose felt a wave of dread in her chest. But when Mama got close, she could see a little smile on her face.

"Well, we have our first contract sale," she said brightly. "Twenty-five barrels! But he says we must have the barrels ready by tomorrow. The scoundrel wanted to give only one dollar fifty cents a barrel! And the barrels costing us fifteen cents apiece!"

"What'd you settle on, then?" Mr. Stubbins asked eagerly.

"Two dollars fifteen cents," Mama said, looking at him with hope in her eyes. "It isn't too low, do you think?"

"Them buyers drive a hard bargain, Mrs. Wilder. I'd say you done yourself about right. We only just got started a-picking. Iffen the whole orchard was colored up, you maybe could've got another ten cents or so. But leastways you know you're a-getting that much out'n your crop."

Rose quickly figured the profit: fifty dollars! The mortgage on the farm was $350, including the extra twenty acres they had bought from a neighbor a few years before. On top of that, there was interest of $35 a year. If they could just sell another hundred barrels at $2.15 each, the farm would be almost theirs, free and clear! And if they could sell 150 barrels more, why, they'd be rich! She began pushing apples again with fresh vigor.

They worked late that evening, until it was too dark to tell the difference between green and red apples. Mr. Stubbins had packed ten barrels for Mr. Endicott. They started again early the next morning. The sky had cleared, and bright sunshine warmed the cool fall air. They worked as hard and fast as they could, stopping at dinnertime only long enough to wolf down their food.

Mr. Stubbins was packing the last barrel in the afternoon when two big wagons came to take them away. Mr. Endicott paid Mama and Papa, and Papa rode straightaway into town to put that money in the bank. That was too much to carry in his pocket and worry about losing.

No other contract buyers came for several days. Local farmers came to buy culls and some number twos. They bought mostly bushels, not whole barrels. Mama could get only about thirty-five cents a bushel for the seconds, and twenty cents for culls.

Even so, the rattle of a wagon coming up the hill had become music to their ears, more beautiful than a mockingbird's song, more cheerful than sleigh bells.

When the contract buyers finally came, the first picking was done and everyone had gone back into the tops of the trees to pick again. The orchard had been well thinned out, the yellowing leaves blew in the wind, and the ground beneath the trees was littered with falls and rots.

Twenty-five barrels of number ones and thirty barrels of number twos sat in the shade, along with twenty barrels of culls. But the price had kept falling every day. The buyers wouldn't budge above $1.45 a barrel for number ones, and Mama and Papa had to let some of them go for as little as $1.30.

By the time the orchard had been picked over a second time and the last buyers came, the price had dropped again, to just $1.05 a barrel for number ones. The last barrels went for eighty-five cents.

Finally one day the orchard was bare of fruit and leaves. The pickers went home, taking twenty-five barrels altogether for their share. They had harvested 173 barrels of apples. Mama, Papa, and Rose were exhausted, and it was dispiriting to come home to two weeks of undone housework.

Papa sat at the supper table that night, working his figures with a pencil while Mama and Rose cleaned up. Every so often Mama would peer over his shoulder and make a comment: "Don't forget those five barrels we set aside for ourselves," or "Didn't Reynolds give a dollar twenty cents for those number twos?" After a long time, Papa sat back and lit his pipe.

"Well, we aren't rich yet, by a long shot," he said. "We took in one hundred thirty-seven dollars and forty cents. After the cost of the barrels, that's about one hundred twenty dollars clear money."

"Well, maybe next year we will catch the market higher," Mama said, brushing the crumbs from the tablecloth. "But it just seems the farmer always gets the short end of the thing. I know those contract buyers are getting a big price for our apples in the cities."

"A good crop never brings good prices," Papa said matter-of-factly. "And a poor crop never brings good money. That's farming. You have to keep everlasting at it."

Rose sighed as she sat down to finish her cup of tea.

"Don't you fret, Rose," Papa said, pointing the stem of his pipe at her. "We aimed for the stars, but we've still got our feet right on the ground."

"But Papa, it just doesn't seem fair, after we worked so hard," Rose complained. "You wanted so much to pay off the mortgage, and to build up the farm, and move back to it. Now it'll be another year of paying interest, and who knows how long before it's paid off."

Papa chuckled. "Why, Rose, you're getting to sound like the woman of the house."

Mama gave Papa a tired smile.

"But you ought to give a look to the bright side. We've paid the mortgage down some, we have the next year to look forward to, and apples coming out our ears."

Rose had to laugh. But inside her this question gnawed: How much longer must they strive and work before they could have their dreams? How long did it take for a person to get where he or she wanted to be? Mama and Papa had been reaching out for their dream all their lives. But as far as Rose could see, the closer they got, the harder it was to grasp.

The Man with the Hoe

In November Mr. McKinley won the election to stay on as president for four more years. Mr. Roosevelt became the new vice president. The old one, Mr. Hobart, had taken ill and died.

Papa said it was strange how folks liked Mr. Roosevelt so much better than the President. Mr. Roosevelt had a nickname, Teddy, and the newspapers said he was a hero in the war with Spain in Cuba. He had traveled all across the country before the election, even to Missouri, making speeches and asking for votes. The cartoons always showed him with big teeth, grinning fearlessly, and his hands clenched into fists like a boxer ready to take on the world.

Papa said fat old Mr. McKinley stayed in Washington, D.C., in the White House, or at his home in Ohio, smoking fifty-cent cigars and letting the trusts run the country. The trusts were big companies that controlled the railroads, meat, flour, matches—just about everything that folks needed to get along.

One trust, Standard Oil, owned practically all the oil in America, Papa said. That was a monopoly. Standard Oil could make people pay any price it wanted for coal oil, and no one could say anything about it. The newspaper cartoonists showed the monopoly trusts as octopuses with their tentacles reaching out and strangling everything in their reach while the little man huddled in the corner starving.

A man from San Francisco, Edwin Markham, had written a poem about the little man. It had been in all the newspapers again and again. Everyone had an opinion of it, and some people had learned it by heart. Reverend Mays even used it for a sermon one Sunday.

Mr. Markham had seen a painting of a poor, beaten-down farmer with his hoe. He sat right down and wrote his poem, "The Man with the Hoe."

Bowed by the weight of centuries he leans
Upon his hoe and gazes on the ground,
The emptiness of ages in his face,
And on his back the burden of the world.

Time's tragedy is in that aching stoop;
Through this dread shape humanity betrayed,
Plundered, profaned and disinherited,
Cries protest to the Judges of the World,
A protest that is also prophecy.

Many a handkerchief blossomed in church the day Reverend Mays read the whole poem aloud. Mr. Markham's words cried out against greed, against the cruelties of lords and rulers toward the common people.

"How will the Future reckon with this Man?
How answer his brute question in that hour
When whirlwinds and rebellion shake the
world?"

Everyone knew without having to be told that the Judges of the World were also the men who owned the trusts. The poem predicted that one day the common people would rise up against them.

Even Rose felt her eyes brim with unshed tears as Reverend Mays read. The poem rang with the most beautiful language that flew to her heart and stuck there like an arrow. The poem was about the suffering of living. How many a poor farmer had she seen, even Papa, bending over his own hoe in his corn patch, the burden of the world on his back?

Rose was fascinated by the power of just a few words. Not only for telling stories, for amusement or to learn something useful, words could change people. It could help them remember something they forgot, and make them feel something they hadn't felt before.

That poem also made Rose mad. She'd read that the trust men who made so much money from their monopolies were spending millions of dollars to build magnificent castles to live in. The newspapers called those men robber barons. Even though they lived like kings, the robber barons still had so much money left they couldn't possibly spend it in three lifetimes.

It didn't seem fair to Rose, but no one could do anything about it because Mr. McKinley was a friend to the trusts.

That's why Papa and Mama hadn't liked Mr. McKinley for the election. Mama couldn't vote, but she and Papa held the same opinion. They had liked Mr. Bryan, who called himself a Populist, and was the candidate of the Democratic Party. Mr. McKinley was a Republican. Everyone had said Mr. Bryan was for the common people, foursquare for the farmers and the workers, and deadset against the trusts.

Rose liked him, too. He was a wonderful

speech-maker, and said things that Rose had thought herself. Mr. Bryan had said that without the farmer, the great cities would starve.

But President McKinley won anyway.

"Well, folks vote with their pocketbooks," Papa said. "Times are good and McKinley's promise of four more years of the 'full dinner pail' must've sat well."

On December 5, 1900, Rose turned fourteen. Once again she took account of herself and how her life had changed. Although it would be a year or so before she could wear long skirts, she was all but a young lady now. She hardly ever went barefoot anymore and hated to be seen by anyone but Mama in her chore dress and apron.

In her heart she was still a country girl, even though she'd been living in town for three years. She enjoyed taking the cow out to pasture at the edge of town each morning, and she was delighted to find a walking-stick bug or hear the cooing of mourning doves. Nothing compared with a stroll through the orchard in the spring when the blossoms sweetened every breath of air and all the branches quivered with bees.

In Rose's mind, though, she was truly a town girl now. She couldn't wait to hear the gossip that always flew after church. There were entertainments to look forward to: the literaries, debates, picnics, Fourth of July, Christmas pageants, and skating parties at Wolf Creek.

Even the noise of a door slamming in the neighborhood, a passing train, the whistle at the flour mill—all the sounds and activities of town connected her to the busy, changing, growing world.

Books gave her another connection. She still read every chance she had, and had read many books borrowed from Mrs. Rippee across the street. As much as she liked her Sunday afternoon walks with Blanche, she didn't mind staying at home in her attic room, reading, or sitting with Mrs. Rippee hearing her stories of days gone past, or discussing the articles she'd read in the newspapers.

Rose could discuss many things with Mama, but it was never the same as with Mrs. Rippee. Mama still seemed to see Rose as a child. There were times Rose was sure Mama hadn't even noticed that she was practically a grown-up girl.

Mrs. Rippee treated her as a grown-up. Sitting in her parlor among her forest of geraniums, she listened to Rose so patiently. She never interrupted and always had a pleasant smile. She never told Rose she had a wrong idea, and she always had something thoughtful to say on any subject. She had become a great friend, and Rose often thought of her as a sort of grandmother.

Rose felt pity for her, too. Mrs. Rippee had grandchildren to fuss over, but she didn't see them much. And Mr. Rippee was away quite a lot, tending to his law business in Hartville, at the courthouse. Mrs. Rippee was lonely, and, Rose realized, so was she.

She had discovered another connection to the world. Since Paul had gone away to work, Rose had become a regular letter writer. She had become accustomed to writing down her thoughts. This made her turn a bit inward, thinking more about who she was, and what she believed.

She sent many letters to Paul. He had come home only once, and only for one day, on his way to his new position in Illinois. Rose hardly had a moment to speak to him, he was so busy visiting with his mother and George. He looked so handsome and prosperous in a new suit and vest, with a silver fob for his father's watch. Seeing him made her miss him more than ever, and she was glad when he kissed her on the cheek before he got on the train to Illinois.

Rose also wrote often to her aunts and grandparents back in De Smet, South Dakota. She hadn't seen them in more than six years, almost half her life. She remembered them, of course, and had many pictures in her mind of having lived among them. She had stayed with Grandma and Grandpa Ingalls, and Mama's sisters, for a long spell while Mama and Papa were mending from diphtheria.

She would always remember pleasant days spent with Grandma and Aunt Mary, sewing or reading. And she would never forget the last night she and Mama and Papa spent in De Smet, when the whole family gathered on the front porch listening to Grandpa play his fiddle.

Rose remembered the dusty summers on the prairie, the bitter cold winters, and the fierce winds that ceaselessly scoured the flat, grassy plains. She had been just a child then. Those times often seemed so far in the past, dreamlike in their blurriness. But through the stories Mama liked to tell about her own childhood growing up on the prairie, Rose's family had stayed dear to her and alive in her imagination.

Now she discovered the pleasure of trading letters with them. She especially enjoyed writing to Aunt Mary, Mama's oldest sister, who was blind. Aunt Mary wrote in Braille, with a special template and a stylus that made raised dots on paper, a different pattern for each letter. Rose had gotten so clever at reading Braille with her eyes closed that she hardly ever had to peek to see if her fingertips had guessed the right letter.

The news from South Dakota was not so interesting. Aunt Mary was old-fashioned and didn't care to write gossip about things that happened in De Smet.

Mostly she wrote about weather, crops, and family news: Grandpa Ingalls had been sickly on and off, and didn't get around so much anymore. He had given up his work selling insurance and stayed mostly at home.

Grandma Ingalls was well, except for a touch of the rheumatism in her hands. Mama's youngest sister, Aunt Grace, was keeping company with a farmer from a nearby town. It was a sure bet that wedding bells weren't far off. Aunt Carrie, the second youngest of the four sisters, had taken up tennis and even had her picture in the newspaper.

It was strange when Aunt Mary wrote

Mama's true name, Laura, in her letters. Everyone but Rose and Papa called her Laura. Her full name was Laura Elizabeth. But Papa had a sister named Laura. So when he and Mama married, he said he would call her Bess, short for Elizabeth.

Rose had begun to write to Aunt Eliza Jane, too. She was an older sister to Papa. Eliza Jane lived in Louisiana, in a town called Crowley that was in a rice-growing district. Rose had met her only a few times, many years before. She knew her hardly at all. But Eliza Jane wrote Rose such an interesting long letter for Rose's fourteenth birthday that Rose had to answer with a long letter of her own. After that they began to write to each other about once a month.

Eliza Jane was very different from Mama's family. Her letters also had family news, but they were rich with gossip. She had been widowed by an older, rich gentleman who had left her with a young boy to raise. But the man's other children, from his first wife who had died, had taken away all the money. It was monstrously unfair, Eliza Jane wrote, but the law in Louisiana was peculiar. She even had to give up her wedding ring.

"It is only a matter of time before we women have the full vote," she wrote. "And when we do, many of the injustices of this world will have the chance for a cure."

No matter how ordinary the news in any letter might be, Rose's spirits always soared whenever Papa came home to dinner and dropped on the kitchen table an envelope addressed to her. In time she began to receive and send so much mail that Mama complained of the cost.

"You spent twenty cents on postage last month, Rose," Mama said, looking up from her account book one night. "What could you possibly have to say in all those letters?"

But Rose knew Mama was just as eager as she to hear the news of the family. When Aunt Mary wrote that Grace might be married, Mama clapped her hands with delight.

"Little Grace!" she cried out. "All grown up and keeping company with a fellow. I can hardly believe it!" Grace was the youngest of the four sisters. Mama still thought of her as the baby.

When Rose read aloud that Grandpa wasn't feeling well and had given up his work, Mama fell silent. The rest of that day, and for a day or so after, her thoughts seemed to be elsewhere, adrift on a faraway ocean.

In school Rose was to have moved up to the Sixth Reader classroom, but the school board had stopped calling them readers. Now the students were divided by grades. Rose was put in the eighth grade, along with students in seventh and ninth grades. Those three grades together were called the high school. She still had boring Professor Bland for her teacher and would until she graduated in two years.

School was longer, too, from September until May, and there was only one session, instead of two as there had been before. But most of the farm children still did not come to school until the harvest was finished in November. They left in March when spring plowing and planting began. There were not so many students in Professor Bland's classroom as in the others. Many of the older boys and girls stayed home to help with chores.

Rose was one of those students. She lived in town, but she was often needed out on the farm, or at home with Mama. Even though she missed some months of the session, when she did go to school she was still ahead of the others in her grade.

Because she did not go to school the whole year with them, and because she often stayed home out of spitefulness toward Professor Bland, she could never truly be one of them. By the time she started attending after the harvest, the classroom had become a family without her.

Blanche was Rose's only friend in school. They called each other best of friends, but in her heart Rose knew she and Blanche were very different. Blanche had no interest in books or the great changes that were sweeping across the country. She lived for gossip, and she had even been walked home from church. Jessie Gaskill had asked her twice.

"He's very sweet, really. But he's awfully dull," Blanche complained. "He has nothing at all to say."

So at recess Rose would stand at the edge of the circle of girls gossiping, near to Blanche, but she almost never spoke up. In class she had to sit wherever she could find an empty seat, often next to one of the country girls no one cared to sit with because they came to school smelling of the barnyard.

Two of the boys in her class were Nate Baird and George Cooley. Nate had stopped bothering Rose after church, and they had become sociable again. George had calmed down some, but he and Rose never had been friends. The rest of the boys were too young and foolish to interest Rose, and the older ones were already fussing over other girls.

But Rose knew none of that mattered anyway. She was not pretty enough for the boys she might care about. Her features were too large, her forehead too high. She longed for tiny, pretty features, large brown eyes, a low forehead with curling hair.

The eyes she saw in the mirror of Mama's chifforobe were gray, and the hair was straight and brown. Not even a pretty, light brown, like Mama's, it was almost black. She had desperately wanted to be pretty, but she knew she never would.

She did have Paul to think of. She could talk with him about anything at all, and he would be interested. She knew their friendship was true, and she believed with all her heart that he would come back to Mansfield. Then everything would change for her. Everything.

In the spring there had been a late frost that nipped the apple blossoms in their buds. It was terrible news, because it meant most of the orchard trees couldn't set any fruit that year. Papa said they would be lucky to get forty barrels, and who could say if any might be number ones?

That summer was hot and dry, and seemed to stretch out forever. Rose felt a growing restlessness that she couldn't explain, and it wouldn't go away. Home was cozy, and life flowed on as peaceful and serene as ever. But somehow the days had begun to run together into one long day that had been her entire life, a life of chores and rules and manners—and loneliness.

That May, Blanche graduated from high school. In September, she was to go away to attend an academy in Mountain Grove, a bigger town about twenty miles to the east of Mansfield. She would live there during the week, and come home on weekends.

"What's an academy?" Rose wanted to know. The two girls sat after Sunday supper on the wide porch of Blanche's house, on wicker chairs with soft cushions. It was a hot evening in August. Cicadas shrilled in the trees, and from inside the house came the clattering sounds of Edwinna finishing the dishes.

"I'm not sure," Blanche said, cooling herself with a paper fan from church. "It's a higher school than high school. I'll have to study Latin and algebra and geometry. I wish I didn't. Who cares for any of that? But Mother and Father said what'll I do, sitting around the house all the time. They think I ought to better myself, and get to know a better class of people."

Rose plucked the collar of her dress, to get some fresh air against her skin. Even though the sun was setting, the heat pressed down like a pot lid.

"It sounds wonderful," Rose said. "To learn a language. And maybe you'll have a beau at the academy."

Suddenly Rose wanted more than anything to go to the Mountain Grove Academy with Blanche. It sounded so grown-up and sophisticated.

"Maybe Mama and Papa would let me go when I graduate. Then we could be in the same school again."

"Oh, I wish you could," Blanche said, leaning forward, her face lighting up. Then she slumped back and the light went out. "But . . . I don't know."

"What?" Rose demanded.

"It costs a great deal," said Blanche sheepishly.

"How much?"

"I oughn't say. It isn't polite to speak of money."

"*Blanche!* How much?"

"Well, Father said with board and tuition, and train fares back home on the weekends"—Blanche bit her lip—"well, it might be twenty dollars a month."

Rose gasped. "Every month?"

Blanche nodded, grimacing.

Rose sank heavily back into the chair. Twenty dollars a month! The whole nine months of school would cost one hundred and eighty dollars. They hadn't even made that much from the whole first crop of apples! It was too much to even think about asking Mama and Papa.

Rose looked over at Blanche and sighed. Blanche shrugged. "It'll probably be awful anyway," she said quietly. "And I'll see you every weekend. That's for certain."

Rose regretted asking. It only reminded them both how different her life was from Blanche's. It only helped remind Rose of the constant struggle Mama and Papa faced just to hold on to what they had.

Rose's spirits sank with each step of her walk back home that evening. Her world, the world of the little town in the Ozarks, was shrinking, while the world beyond was growing and changing. The two people she cared for most after Mama and Papa, Paul and Blanche, had the chance to see that world. And they were leaving her behind.

The Most Awful News

Shortly after Blanche left to start at the academy, Rose was out on the farm one bright Friday, helping with the corn harvest. When she and Mama and Papa headed back to town in the wagon, they heard the church bells ringing, and the whistle at the flour mill was wailing.

"Sounds like something big's up," said Papa, chirruping to the horses to get them trotting. "Hope it isn't a fire."

When the wagon crested the hill that led down into town, they could see knots of people in the street. As they passed the schoolhouse at the edge of town, a little boy ran up to the wagon, waving his hat and shouting, "They shot him! They shot him!"

Papa reined in the horses, and the wagon creaked to a stop. "Shot who, son? Who shot who? Make some sense."

"It's the President, mister. Somebody's gone and shot him!"

"Oh, no!" Mama cried out.

"Tarnation," Papa growled.

Rose, sitting on the seat between them, felt a wave of panic race up her spine. Papa quickly drove the horses up to the hitching rail in front of the house. He jumped down and tied up the team. Then he helped Mama and Rose down from the seat.

Mrs. Rippee came rushing across the street, her handkerchief in her hand, her cheeks wet. A strand of her tidy silver hair had come undone and floated in the air.

"Oh, Mrs. Wilder," she wept. "It's the most awful news. Some man, an anarchist, they say, shot poor Mr. McKinley. The wires say he's likely to die. Oh, what is this terrible world coming to? Three presidents in forty years!"

Then tears flooded Rose's eyes. She wasn't sure why, but she felt a terror greater than any she'd ever known. The earth seemed to have split open, and it threatened to swallow them all. The President of the United States! Of course, Rose had studied in school about the murders of President Lincoln and President Garfield.

But those terrible things had happened years before. They were history. It was unthinkable that anyone should really want to do such a thing again. Then she remembered with cold horror reading in a newspaper that some people hated McKinley so much they said he should be killed. Now someone had actually gone and tried it.

For the next week life in Mansfield slowed nearly to a halt. That Sunday Reverend Mays made his whole sermon a prayer that the President would mend. The next week school was canceled. Every morning a crowd gathered at the depot to catch the latest wires.

The Most Awful News

At first the reports said the President was gravely ill, shot through the stomach. But after a few days, he was feeling a little better, and even asked for a cigar.

No newspapers were left in the depot waiting room, so Rose had to scour the town to find one. She read Mr. Coday's newspaper at Blanche's house, and Mrs. Rippee's. But no one would give theirs up for anything.

"Mind you don't wrinkle it," Blanche said as they pored over her father's *Chicago Interocean*. "Papa wants to keep it, for a souvenir."

The shooting of the President filled nearly every page. The President had been visiting the Pan-American Exposition in Buffalo, New York. A young man named Leon Czolgosz had hidden a derringer in a bandage he had wrapped around his hand.

The President had been shaking hands in a crowd when Mr. Czolgosz walked up and shot him through the false bandage. The President had been brave, gasping to his secretary, "My wife, be careful about her; don't let her know."

The crowd began to strike Mr. Czolgosz, but the President told them, "Let no one hurt him." The newspapers said Mr. Czolgosz was an anarchist. That was a person who believed there should be no government at all. Some anarchists believed it was right to kill the leader of any government.

Rose had read enough history to know that anarchy made no sense. How could people live if everyone did whatever they liked?

Now, because of an idea that made no sense, the President lay in a hospital bed fighting for his life. Rose felt terrible about not liking Mr. McKinley. No matter how much he was for the wealthy interests, it was a dreadful thing to take the life of another, and a cowardly thing to try to kill the President of the United States while he was just being sociable. What was the world coming to?

One week and a day after President McKinley was shot, early in the morning before sunup when the town was just waking,

Rose was splashing cold water on her face at the basin by the back door when the whistle at the flour mill began to shriek. Mama paused in the middle of stuffing wood in the cookstove. The back door flew open, and Papa came hurriedly in from milking.

"Do you think . . . ?" Mama asked anxiously.

"Has to be," Papa said, setting down the pail. "I'll run downtown and see."

The President had died, early that morning. Now the Vice President, Mr. Roosevelt, became the President. It had happened twice before, when John Wilkes Booth killed President Lincoln, and Charles J. Guiteau killed President James A. Garfield. Each time a president died, another person, chosen by the people, stepped right up to lead the country.

That was the way the Founding Fathers had written the Constitution. Even if both the President and the Vice President were to die, the Speaker of the House of Representatives would become the president of the country. If he died, it would be the President Pro Tempore of the Senate. All of those people had been elected by the voters. There were many people after that too, waiting in line if all the others were to die.

No matter who became president that way, the people could get rid of him in the next election.

That was democracy, Rose realized. The anarchists might kill the President, but they could never kill America.

The Awkward Age

Rose turned fifteen that winter, and her restlessness grew until it was unbearable. That spring Mama had become almost an irritation to her. Before she had thought of Mama as always being there, like the weather, unpredictable and a nuisance now and then, but mostly pleasant.

Now Rose began to find her annoying, exasperating. It was as if Mama was determined to keep her from growing up.

"Rose is at the awkward age," Mama said patiently to Mrs. Helfinstine one day as they

sat in the dining room having coffee together.
Rose scowled as she swept a pile of crumbs
up off the kitchen floor. To be talked about as
if she were a mere child!

"Yes, but my land, you never can tell what
they'll turn into," Mrs. Helfinstine chirped
brightly. "It's too soon to lose hope yet." She
turned and looked at Rose through the
kitchen doorway and added, "I wonder at
you, Rose. It's a real pretty dimity, and if your
mother says mutton-leg sleeves, it's mutton-
leg sleeves. I don't know why she stands any
of your lip."

Rose felt a hot flush of anger on the back of
her neck. "I don't want mutton-leg sleeves,"
she all but yelled.

"Rose!" Mama's stern tone of voice quelled
her, but still she muttered, "Well, I don't."
She didn't have the courage to add aloud,
"And I won't have them!" She argued to herself, "It's my dress, isn't it? I have to wear it,
don't I? I guess if I want mousquetaire
sleeves I have a right."

Mousquetaire sleeves would take two more yards of dimity for each sleeve, and that cost twenty cents. But the real problem was that the only woman in town who had a mousquetaire sleeve pattern was Mrs. Beaumont. Mama said she could not pay for a pattern, especially after the second apple harvest had been so poor.

The Beaumonts were rich. Mr. Beaumont owned the bank. Mrs. Beaumont's house and her clothes were the finest in town. She was a member of the Eastern Star with Mama, but Mama would have died of hunger rather than accept a scrap of charity from her. Mama just plain didn't like Mrs. Beaumont, or her oldest daughter, Lois. They had snooped around in Miss Sarah's business with Wade Tucker, and Lois had pulled that mean trick on Paul at the pie supper years before.

Rose felt she had enough to bear in her life without looking like a poor country waif. All the other girls would be wearing the latest style in sleeves that summer. Elsa Beaumont's best dress was to be China silk. The Hibbard twins were having organdy made up over pink silkaleen, and Blanche had a pale-green silk mousseline.

Day after day Rose pleaded with Mama. She argued, she coaxed, she finally broke down and shed tears.

"Why can't I ever have anything like other girls? It isn't my fault we're poor! It's only a horrid old five-cent dimity, but I could bear it if only we could make it up in style."

Mama looked at Rose over her glasses with a look of frustration mixed with weariness. "I don't care for you talking to me like that, Rose. Someday you'll have a girl of your own, and if you're poor . . ."

She bent back to the skirt-gores in her lap and went on hurriedly basting them together. Then she sighed heavily and said, without looking up, "Well, go on then. Go and ask Mrs. Beaumont."

"Oh, Mama, thank you," Rose said, trying not to sound triumphant. She flew to change her dress and shoes and put on her felt hat with the polka-dot band. Then she dashed out the front door, letting the screen slam behind her.

Springtime was in the air. The muddy street steamed. All the yards were filmed with green, and only scraps of dirty snow remained on the shady side of woodpiles and under the edge of the board sidewalk.

Rose was so happy she could hardly bear it. But in her happiness she promised herself she would never forget her sufferings. When she was married, all her children would always be beautifully dressed. They would want for nothing.

From the gate she waved to Mrs. Rippee, watching from her parlor window across the street. The sunshine was warm; the treetops were knobby with swollen buds. Mares grazed in the livery-stable pasture, their gangling colts cavorting around them.

Rose walked haughtily past the boys scuffling in front of the livery stable and looked up the east side of the square. She saw that the new spring dress goods were coming to

Reynolds' Store. Papa's draywagon was backed up to the sidewalk. Papa had wound the lines around the whip and was unloading boxes. Inside the doorway one of Mr. Reynolds' clerks, Tom Blanchard, was prying off the tops.

"Hello, kid!" Tom called out to her. "Come and have a look at 'em!"

Tom was the most popular clerk in the store, even more than Mr. Reynolds himself. The women all asked for him, because he was a steady, dependable young man who worked hard and saved his money and always had a cheerful word for everyone. No one minded his badly patched shirts and the nail he used to fasten one suspender to his trousers.

Rose stepped up onto the boardwalk and into the store as Tom ripped the last board off a case. He began lifting bolts of goods to the counter.

"Pretty, ain't they?" he said with pride. All along the counter, organdies and muslins and Persian lawns were piled high. The whole place bloomed with their freshness. With a fingertip Rose touched a sheer white sprinkled with flowers.

"Spring's here, all right," Tom said.

Rose knew what he meant. There was no way to say it, but it was there—in the delicately colored and snowy fabrics, in the air that smelled of grass and damp earth, in the jingle of bits when the horses shook their heads, and in the lilt of someone's whistling. The hammering at the blacksmith shop sounded like bells. There was a shimmer in just being alive.

Papa strolled in, lifting his hat to wipe his brow and balding head with his handkerchief.

"What're you doing uptown?" he asked. Papa spoke kindly, but Rose knew he was thinking there was plenty of work she could be doing at home, and that nice girls didn't loiter around the store. So she continued on her errand, casting a last yearning glance at the bouquet of colored bolts piled on the counter.

Rose's stomach fluttered as she opened the gate and walked up the path to the Beaumonts' house. It stood back from the street in a big yard. On the lawn were two iron deer that always looked startled and a little rusty. The house was two-storied, with bay windows and a tall eight-sided cupola on top. Colored glass panes surrounded the bay windows and the heavy front door, which had a ground-glass scene of deer and trees set into it, and a polished round-bellied brass doorknob.

Rose did not have to twist the handle of the bell. The door stood open to the long hall, and a sewing machine hummed in the dining room. The sound was hurried and harassed. Mrs. Beaumont had five girls and herself to dress. As rich as they were, Mr. Beaumont didn't approve of ready-made dresses that could be bought out of a mail-order catalogue. He said the merchants in town were his customers, and his family, at least, would show a little respect and keep their trade right there in town. So Mrs. Beaumont had more sewing than any other woman in Mansfield.

Rose stepped almost on tiptoe into the grand foyer, and then through the dining-room door. Bolts of longcloth and Swiss embroidery lay on the dining-room chairs. Patterns and fashion plates, whalebones, cards of lace and buttons and hooks-and-eyes lay everywhere. Elsa was turning and preening before the tall pier-glass. She spotted Rose in the mirror and swung around.

"Hello, kiddo!" she sang out. That was the new, clever way to greet a friend. "Kid" and "kiddo." Everyone was reading the new colored comics that came with the newspapers now, and imitating the way the characters spoke. Mama didn't approve of such language, and truthfully Rose couldn't make those words come out of her own mouth. But from Elsa, who was so modern and sophisticated in every way, they fell as right as rain.

Rose noticed that Elsa's hair was all done up. Then she saw that the flounces of Elsa's new plaid gingham dress almost touched the floor.

"Why, Elsa Beaumont!" Rose burst out, then quickly she remembered to turn and murmur a proper, "Good morning, Mrs. Beaumont."

Elsa didn't give her mother time to answer. "Like it?" she asked airily. She pulled the belt down smartly in front, smoothed her hips, and swiveled to set her skirts swinging. "Mama, I'm *going* to have rhinestone combs and a barrette to match."

"It's ridiculous," Elsa's mother spat out, tramping hard on the sewing machine treadle to get the needle through a thick seam. "You're not old enough." Elsa was only two months older than Rose.

"You're not old enough." Rose had heard it a thousand times. "I don't think you're old enough for long skirts yet," Mama had said. "You'll be grown up a long time, but you'll only be a girl once." She couldn't see that Rose had come to hate having her bare ankles showing for anyone to see. She was practically a grown woman, and still in short skirts!

Suddenly, with no thought at all, Rose blurted a lie. "*My* mother's putting me into long skirts."

Elsa shot Rose a suspicious glance, one eyebrow arched, and Rose saw that she'd sprung a trap on herself. Now she would have to make Mama do it, or she could never hold her head up again.

"Seems to me you're rushing your age," Mrs. Beaumont said, snapping the thread. She let her hands rest on the heap of petticoat ruffles, and a sad look passed over her face. "My, my, the way you young ones grow up nowadays."

"Well," Elsa retorted pertly, "I guess you'd be sorry if we didn't!" No other girl in town was so quick, so smart as Elsa. Her mother just couldn't do a thing with her, and Rose envied that.

Mrs. Beaumont said she'd be delighted to lend her the mousquetaire sleeve pattern. As she hunted for it, Rose politely answered her questions. Yes, her mother was well, thank you. Old Mrs. Helfinstine was feeling about the same. Yes, the new goods came into Reynolds'. Tom Blanchard was unpacking them when she came by.

"I hear Tom's taking a shine to Minnie Stone," Mrs. Beaumont remarked absently.

"What?" Elsa cried. "Not Minnie Stone. Why . . . why, I don't believe it! As if dear, sweet Tom would take other men's leavings!"

"Don't talk like that, Elsa," Mrs. Beaumont said sharply. "You don't know what you're saying."

But Elsa would not be silenced. "I guess I do so! That Minnie Stone is an old maid if ever there was one, and if that's not men's leavings, what is? And wasn't she engaged twice, and neither of 'em took her? Jilted once is scandal enough, but jilted *twice* . . . my goodness, I don't know what more you'd want against a girl—two broken engagements!"

Rose stood still as a statue, in fascinated shock.

"Minnie's as good as gold to her poor widowed mother," said Mrs. Beaumont. "And whatever happened, you can't tell me there was ever a true word said against poor Minnie. And I'll thank you, miss, to speak with more respect—"

Just then Elsa swooped across the room toward Rose with a mischievous look in her eyes. She grabbed Rose's elbow and swept her along into the foyer.

"Elsa, you come right back here! Elsa!" Mrs. Beaumont called. "Where are you going?"

Elsa called over her shoulder, "I'm only going far's the store with Rose."

"You be right back. And finish those dishes when you do."

"My goodness, Mama, don't nag so!" Elsa shouted impatiently. Rose expected a thunderclap, or something even more terrible. If she'd spoken so to Mama, she might have expected a slap in the face, although Mama had never once struck her.

But nothing happened to Elsa, and in an instant they were free, out the door into the soft sunshine and the breeze that seemed somehow wild and full of joy.

Elsa tucked her arm cozily into Rose's. "That's one thing I'm never, never going to do when I'm married," she declared. "I'm never going to nag my children."

They walked uptown. When they reached the square Rose quickly scanned all four sides to see if Papa was still there. If he was, she would walk straight home. But he wasn't, so they slowly began to walk around it.

"Do you want to know a secret?" Elsa said as they passed Reynolds'.

Rose's head spun, wondering if it could be possible that Elsa Beaumont was choosing her for a friend. Rose crossed her heart and solemnly promised never to tell, never as long as she lived to breathe one word to any living soul, and never, never, not if she were dying, to let Mama even suspect.

Even then Rose had to coax her. But at last Elsa told. She had met a traveling man.

Rose stopped in her tracks and stared at Elsa in disbelief. She didn't know what to say. The letters of the sign on Coday's Drugs seemed to wobble before her eyes.

"His name is Mr. Andrews," Elsa said when Rose could move her feet again. "I call him Andy. Of course, not to his face. He works out of St. Louis. He wears a real diamond ring, and he told me I was the prettiest girl in his whole territory. He's mad about me, simply mad."

Rose could only listen spellbound. She had seen traveling men in town. Everyone did. They came nearly every day on the trains, bringing their order books. They traveled around the country selling things, everything from horse collars to millinery thread. They got off a train one day, and the next day, or even the same day, they got on another and left.

The storekeepers who were their customers knew the traveling men in a business way. And Papa hauled their heavy sample cases in his draywagon and knew their names. But no respectable man would join in the card games they played until all hours, and for money, too.

There was a glamour about those city men who came and went without being known. They stayed overnight at the Mansfield Hotel, paying a whole dollar, an awesome extravagance. Rose saw them sometimes through the hotel windows, sitting in the shabby chairs among the brass spittoons, legs flung over chair arms, thumbs in the armholes of their vests, derby hats pushed back on their heads and fat, gold-banded cigars cocked in the corners of their mouths.

Rose always hurried past, her eyelids lowered. Traveling men were bold, bad, and wickedly dangerous. Every mother told every daughter the same thing. Girls who knew traveling men were not girls that nice girls knew.

Traveling men had been everywhere. They had seen everything. They wore boiled shirts and stiff collars every day. Their shoes gleamed with polish. Rings twinkled on their fingers. Glittering watch chains looped across their fancy vests.

They came from the big wicked cities, and then they went back to them. Traveling men were not to be trusted.

"And Rose," Elsa dreamily murmured in her ear. "Oh, Rose, it's true love at last! I know it is, because—don't ever tell—" She whispered, "I love him."

Rose's feet could hardly find the sidewalk. "Elsa!" she gasped. "What—what does it feel like?"

Elsa said it was wonderful. Slowly the two girls walked around the square. Elsa told what he said, what she said, what she thought, and what she thought he thought because of what he'd said. Rose held the mousquetaire sleeve pattern in a feverish grip. She knew Mama was long past expecting her, but she couldn't tear herself away. It was incredible that Elsa Beaumont, of all girls, was confiding such a secret to her.

Finally Rose said good-bye and dashed home. Mama was putting out dinner, and Papa, already washed, was combing his hair before the little mirror on the kitchen wall. He looked at Rose sternly, and Mama closed the door to the dining room where two boarders, traveling ministers, waited for their meal.

"You see to it, young lady that you're here to help get dinner after this," Mama chided as she poured the gravy into its pitcher. "I've been sewing on your dress all morning, and Papa tells me you were gadding about the streets with Elsa Beaumont."

Rose's face blazed with shame.

Mama set the pot of gravy back on the stove with a clatter. "Don't let me catch you dawdling away precious time again, with your chores going wanting."

"No, Mama," Rose murmured.

"Now fill up those water glasses and be quick about it."

At dinner Mama and Papa talked about setting out the tomato plants, and about taking down the heater stove. The ministers talked about the fine weather. The doors and windows were open, letting the sweet air flow through the house. Soon violets would bloom along the country roads, and buttercups and dandelions in the vacant lots.

Rose's serge dress felt stuffy on her, but she had outgrown last summer's dresses. Mama would want to let down their hems again, but Rose knew desperately that she *must* have long skirts.

As soon as dinner was over and Papa and the ministers had left, Rose began her pleading. Mama was firm. "It makes no difference to me that Elsa Beaumont is going into long skirts. She is no example for you or anybody."

"Why, Mama?" Rose complained. To her, no other girl could compare to Elsa. It was not just that she was pretty and dressed so stylishly. She had an air. She was never shy or awkward, never at a loss. She always had something to say to the boys, and she always knew what to do.

"She's just plain boy-crazy," Mama said. "I wonder she hasn't been talked about before this."

Rose sprang to Elsa's defense. "She isn't either boy-crazy." Mama glared at her. "Oh, I'm sorry, Mama," Rose said quickly. "Honest, I didn't mean to contradict. But how can Elsa help it if all the boys are crazy about her?"

That was what Elsa had said. "Can I help it if they're all crazy about me?" she had asked airily. She had said it in a charming, pert way, tilting her chin and swishing her skirts. "They can just *be* crazy, for all of me! Twenty-three skiddoo for them!"

When Rose saw Elsa glance at a boy, she

felt excited, embarrassed, and bitter. She couldn't look at a boy like that. Elsa bewitched boy after boy, and Rose hadn't yet even got one steady beau. All she had was Paul, as a friend, and he was far away.

"Maybe boys will be foolish about a girl like that," Mama said. "But when it comes to marrying, they pick out a good sensible, worthy girl. Elsa Beaumont is rushing her age, and you mark my words: One of these days she'll find herself on the shelf. Look what happened to her sister Lois, after the business with that boy from Seymour."

The trouble was, Rose didn't want to be a sensible, worthy girl. She wanted to be like Elsa. But she could never tell that to Mama.

So Rose spoke of her feelings of modesty. She blushed, and so did Mama. Looking away, Rose muttered, "I'm too big, Mama. I can't let people—boys—see my lower limbs. It just isn't decent!"

Rose felt herself becoming frantic, but she couldn't stop the words from rushing out. "If you won't let me have decent clothes, I'll just have to . . . I can't go anywhere! I'll just have to stay home and hide. Oh Mama, please, *please*!"

Mama looked at Rose thoughtfully for a moment, her chin in her hand. Then she turned and took her apron down from its hook by the backdoor.

"I don't know how on earth I can," she said. "It means all new goods." She sighed, and began to tie the apron strings. "Well, maybe I can inset gores and put a scalloped flounce on your piqué. And I can get along with my last summer's lawn, I suppose."

Rose hardly heard the last sentence. The sigh meant Mama had given in. Rose jumped up, and with a joyous clatter she began to scrape and stack the dishes.

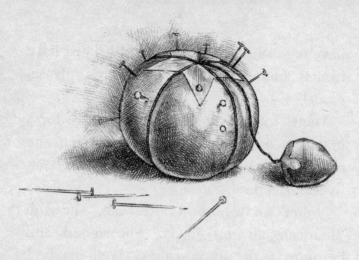

Snookums and Buster

Rose came in the front door. She had returned Mrs. Helfinstine's umbrella, which Mama had borrowed the day before to walk home in the rain. Dress patterns on the floor skittered in the breeze. Mama, on her knees, went on taking pins from her mouth and marking the rows of perforations in the enormous mousquetaire sleeve pattern she had copied from Mrs. Beaumont's.

When her mouth was empty, she said, "Rose, it's going to take four yards more, and

I'll have to have fifteen yards of beading and black velvet ribbon to run through it."

Rose got down on her knees, too, and helped hold the paper in place. Mama's forehead was grooved with worry, and it took Rose a little time to think of an excuse for going to Elsa's. At last she said, "Mama, when I go for the extra goods, I'll take back the sleeve pattern."

"That's my thoughtful girl," Mama said, pleased. "It does go against the grain to be beholden to Mrs. Beaumont a minute longer than I can help. Remember your manners, now, and thank her nicely."

Rose didn't dare dally at the Beaumonts' this time, or try to sneak away for a walk with Elsa. But she just had to know more about her traveling man, Mr. Andrews. She made Elsa promise to walk with her on Sunday, after dinner.

On Sunday, the dimity wasn't finished. Rose had to wear her winter best to church. She hated that dress. It was her old, short, navy-blue serge with pink baby-ribbon edging its

satin yoke and cuffs. Elsa was lovely in pale-blue muslin and a leghorn hat smothered in roses.

They met at the western end of the square. The earth was still moist at the grass roots, and the crossings were muddy.

They walked slowly up and down the long boardwalk that went toward the cemetery. Trees arched over it. The shadows of their branches quivered on the boards, and looking up Rose saw the mist of color against the shimmering sky. The day was still with a Sunday stillness. Far away on the farms, a dog barked and a hen cackled. The rustle of their petticoats seemed stylishly loud.

They gossiped about Tom and Minnie. Elsa said Tom would never marry Minnie, "and there's no three ways about it!"

Finally, Elsa talked about Mr. Andrews. She had met him in Coday's Drugs. She had been buying a nickel's worth of sulphur to take for her complexion, and he was just standing there at the counter.

"It seems so providential to me," Elsa said.

"Honestly, Buster, doesn't it seem to you as if it was meant to be?" Rose tried to hide her dislike of that nickname. Buster Brown was a character in the funny papers. Rose liked Buster Brown, but she didn't think it was a pretty-sounding name for a girl, and she didn't care for anyone to call her that. But with Elsa she kept her thoughts to herself.

Elsa said she wasn't expecting anything at all; she just kind of happened to glance at Mr. Andrews. And he was looking at her! So of course, she looked right away from him.

"But he kept looking and looking at me. But of course I didn't pay any attention at all. But I must have just kind of glanced his way, or something, because he said, 'Hello, Snookums!'"

Rose guffawed.

"Wasn't that strange?" Elsa said, leaning close to Rose. "Honestly, Buster, don't you think that's the strangest thing?"

It was, because Elsa had been called Snookums ever since the young people of Mansfield had started reading the Sunday funny papers. But he didn't know that. And yet he said, "Hello, Snookums!"

"And Buster," Elsa raced on, "I had the queerest feeling. Right that very minute, I knew he was my Fate. Because you know what I believe? I believe that when a girl meets the one man in the whole world that's meant for her, she knows. Because I knew.

"Oh Buster, to think, only two more days and I'll see him again! His route brings him back to town on Number Five, Wednesday night. I've got to see him." Her thin hand clutched Rose's arm. "Buster, you've *got* to come with me somehow. You've *got* to. I can't meet him alone. And it must be secret, but it must seem to be accidental. He's got to think I'm surprised," she explained. "Or he might get the notion that . . . well, that I'm kind of . . . well, easy." She tossed her head, saying with spirit, "He needn't think it's going to be any easy job, getting *me*!"

Rose's head spun from trying to keep up with Elsa's thoughts and plans. It was all so dangerous and wicked, and exciting. Wednesday! Somehow they both would have to try to trick their parents, and then make it appear an accident when they ran into Mr. Andrews.

"But Snookums," Rose said, forcing herself to use Elsa's nickname, "if he's got any sense at all, how can he help guessing—"

"Oh, don't be a boob!" Elsa snapped impatiently. "You know, Buster, I don't think you know how to manage boys."

Her boldness was a thunderclap. Rose hesitated; then she asked humbly, "How do you manage them?"

"Oh, I don't know," Elsa replied airily. "It's just a gift, I guess. Some girls have it, and some just don't. It isn't anything you could learn."

Rose's breath caught in her throat. Her blood ran cold. For the first time it seemed real to her that she could become an old maid. Until that moment such a fate had been like death. It couldn't happen to her.

Rose forced a rough laugh. "Well, I don't care," she said as heartily as she dared. "I don't want to get married. Why, I wouldn't marry the best man on—"

"When I get married," Elsa interrupted dreamily, "I'm going to live in the city and have my own carriage and wear silks and diamonds, and I'm just going to be on the go every single minute. I'm going to be the most popular young matron in society."

Then, as if suddenly remembering Rose, she added, "I'll ask you to come visit me sometimes and you'll see how I dress up to go to parties."

Rose tried to feel grateful, but she couldn't keep a tinge of bitterness out of her thoughts.

"Well," she said finally, "the first thing's to get Mama to let me stay all night with you. And you've just got to come with me, to ask her."

They walked straightaway to Rose's house where, Rose knew, Mama wouldn't say in Elsa's presence what she thought about her, and so she wouldn't say no.

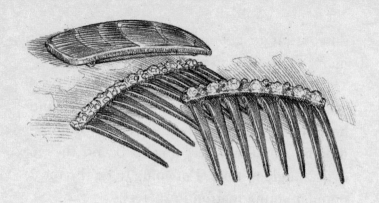

Mr. Andrews

For the next two days Rose was a model daughter, eagerly helpful at home. She swept and dusted without being told, didn't leave a single pot to soak when she did the dishes, and always kept the woodbox full.

After school on Wednesday, she and Elsa burst in on Mama and before she could think of a reason to change her mind, Rose had snatched her nightgown and toothbrush and they were safely out the house.

Elsa squeezed Rose's arm in jubilation. "Well, that's done! I just know everything's going to be all right! I've got a feeling."

The splendor of the Beaumonts' life had become less off-putting to Rose by now. She and Elsa went past the iron deer and the round beds of cannas and followed the path around the bay window to the side porch. A chain bucket pump stood there, and the boards were damp with splashed water.

The rear part of the house was surprisingly untidy. Sewing and toys and garments were scattered everywhere, the furniture was dusty, and Elsa's little sisters made a great racket. In the big kitchen, Mrs. Beaumont was helping the hired girl dish up supper.

"You might get home from school in time to help, once in a while," she said to Elsa. "How do you expect me and Eunice to do everything, with this big house and five young ones on my hands."

"I did the dishes last week," Elsa retorted. "And you can just make the kids do them tonight! I'm not going to, and there's no three ways about it!"

Rose was astounded. She would never have guessed in a thousand years, looking at the serene front of their house, that the Beaumonts lived in such chaos and were so graceless and unpleasant with each other.

Mrs. Beaumont went on quarreling, but did nothing to punish Elsa. In silence Rose took her turn at the basin washing for supper and dried her hands on the draggled roller towel, which looked as if it hadn't been changed in a week.

The supper table groaned with food. Mama set such a table only when company came for Thanksgiving. Elsa didn't even try to eat everything her father put on her plate. Mr. Beaumont, after he mumbled grace, did not say another word.

Everyone ate in muted uneasiness. Rose could see that even Elsa felt a proper awe of her father. At last Mr. Beaumont pushed back his plate, emptied his coffee cup in one long drink, wiped his mustache, and stood up. He walked out, going back to the bank to tend to some late business.

A clamor broke out around the table at once, and Elsa sprang up. "Come along, Buster!" Her sisters whined about the dishes, and she turned on them. "I've got company. I'm not going to do any old dishes and that's flat, and you kids can just lump it!"

"Elsa," Mrs. Beaumont scolded. "I won't have you speaking to your—"

Elsa slammed the door. She and Rose raced the length of the long hall, turned and dashed up the stairs and into Elsa's room. She locked the door, stuffed the keyhole, pulled down the windowshades, and lighted the lamp.

"Now," she said generously, "you can watch me dress up."

Rose gazed around Elsa's room. There were lace curtains on the windows. The wallpaper was covered with large pink roses. The carpet was red and green. The bureau and washstand were old-fashioned, but the big bedstead was gleaming brass. Clothes were flung on the floor, draped on doorknobs.

Tangled things hung from open bureau drawers. The closet bulged with garments hanging on hooks, and fallen from them. Every chair was full. Rose perched on the unmade bed and watched Elsa.

She had sworn she didn't rough her hair. "It's just naturally thick," she'd said. But now Rose saw her roughing it vigorously, strand by strand, with a swift comb. Then she reached under her mattress and pulled out a hair rat and began to pin it to her hair to give it a pompadour.

"Mama would just kill me if she knew," she muttered through hairpins. "But I'm not going to look like an old stick-in-the-mud!"

Finally her pompadour stood up beautifully, just like a Gibson girl's. She coiled the ends and thrust large shell hairpins into the knot. She tucked in rhinestone side combs and clamped a wide tortoiseshell barrette.

"There!" she said, satisfied.

Next Rose helped tighten Elsa's corset, tugging at the strings until she couldn't tighten them another breath. Then Elsa tied the strings of a taffeta petticoat and wriggled into her best dress, a pale-blue silk stylishly flounced and trimmed with yards of black velvet ribbon.

When she had smoothed back the skirt so Rose could hook the placket, and tugged her belt down in front, she looked simply perfect, and Rose said so.

Elsa inspected her reflection in the mirror, bit her lip in thought, then pounced on a small pillow, stripped off the case, and stuffed it into the front of her shirtwaist. With her full, bulging blouse, she looked exactly like a fashion plate.

"Oh, Snookums!" Rose cried, hardly able to bear her envy. "He'll be wild! You're beautiful, just simply beautiful!"

Elsa turned and primped in front of the mirror. "Well, there's no credit to me," she said. "Oh, maybe being stylish is. But being, well, anyway pretty, and popular, and smart, that's only because God made me that way. If he'd made me like you, why then I guess I'd have to be like you, or . . . well, anyway, God can do anything. But I'm honestly not one bit vain, because I don't think men like a girl that's vain, do you?"

"Elsa Beaumont!" Rose gasped. "What are you putting on your face?"

It was a clear liquid from a small bottle. "Epsom salts and water," she told Rose. "It takes the shine off. And Buster, do you know what I'm going to do when I'm married? I'm going to use powder. I am, I don't care! And if people talk about me after I'm married, why, they just can!"

Finally Elsa blew out the lamp and stuck her head out the door to see if anyone was in the hallway. Then she waved for Rose to follow, and they tiptoed fast as they could without making any noise down the stairway. Elsa's silks rustled loudly, but they got downstairs to the front hall before Mrs. Beaumont called, "Elsa? That you?"

The shock stopped Rose for an instant; then she dashed after Elsa. The opening dining-room door let a shaft of lamplight into the hall. Mrs. Beaumont called sharply,

"Elsa! You can't go uptown!"

They escaped out the front door, racing past the iron deer and through the gate. Rose's heart was pounding.

"She can't do anything," Elsa said. "What can she do?"

It was true. Elsa was too big to whip. What *could* her mother do? Stunned, Rose saw that Mama couldn't actually do anything, either. They were free and abroad in the wide, wild night.

The stars were out, but trees cast faint shadows on the long boardwalk. They strolled to the end and back, out again and back, almost to the cemetery and almost to the square.

"He wears a mustache," Elsa said. "Buster, I wonder if it's true, what they say? A kiss without a mustache is like an egg without salt."

"Elsa!" Rose exclaimed. "You wouldn't!"

"Oh, I don't know," she said. "People do."

"But then he wouldn't respect you."

"Well, my goodness, how green do you think I am? It's all right when you're engaged."

"But you aren't engaged," Rose said.

"Oh, don't be such a boob!"

They were both jittery and quivering. They started and clutched each other every other moment, fearful of every shadow, every little noise. Suppose someone recognized them? Suppose Mama learned that Mrs. Beaumont didn't know where they were? Suppose their fathers found out?

They paused by the darkened post office. Lamps burned in Reynolds' Store, Coday's Drugs, the barbershop, the hotel, and the bank. Men stood in the shadows. They could hear their voices and see the red ends of cigars pulsing in the dark. Beyond the square the starry sky came down to the long black depot and the railroad tracks. A switch light glowed red and green.

Rose shivered. Elsa was risking everything for love. But what was Rose risking every-thing for? It was foolish, even crazy. She'd never have thought of doing something so scandalous. But she couldn't desert Elsa now, or lose this chance to watch Elsa and see how she bewitched Mr. Andrews.

When the first faraway shriek of Number Five's whistle reached them from beyond the cut, Elsa gripped Rose's arm.

Now everywhere the darkness stirred. Along the sidewalk men moved, sauntering through the patches of lamplight toward the depot. A burst of noisy voices came from the barbershop. Other men hurried from the livery stable and the drugstore, and the hotel roustabout pushed the baggage cart down the middle of the street. Rose realized Papa would be meeting the train with his draywagon, and that set a flight of butterflies churning in her stomach.

The railroad tracks began to hum, a light glared on the twin steel rails, and the train came roaring into the depot with its bell clanging. A jolting crash of metal, and Number Five was there.

Black shapes of men crowded the depot platform. Above their heads Rose saw the passengers sitting in red velvet seats, in a brilliant light that gleamed on polished wood.

Then the bell began to clang again, lanterns were set swinging, and the engine's great wheels began to turn and spin. Then Number Five roared away into the night, its whistle screaming.

Rose and Elsa fled to the end of the boardwalk, beyond the last house, and waited until no more homecoming men clicked their gates shut behind them. The last window went dark. But Coday's Drugs didn't close until nine o'clock. Elsa was sure Mr. Andrews would go there to buy his cigars.

They sneaked past all the still houses. The only light on the square was at the drugstore. Rose and Elsa waited. Every shadow seemed to have eyes.

The door opened, and a man came out. Rose heard Elsa's breath catch. She nudged Rose and they walked forward. Rose saw that the man was not very tall. He wore a pale vest and a derby hat. Elsa's little shriek made Rose jump.

"My goodness!" she cried softly. "Why, my goodness gracious me, it's Mr. *Andrews*! Why, where on earth did *you* come from? This *is* an unexpected pleasure. How are you?"

Rose had never heard Elsa speak so elegantly.

"Well, well, well, well!" Mr. Andrews said, sounding very pleased. He took the cigar from his mouth, lifted his hat with a flourish, and set it on his head again at a jaunty angle. "Well, well, and how's little bright-eyes?"

"Oh, fine!" Elsa chirped. "Just fine! Fine and dandy!" She laughed a peal of laughter. It sounded more silvery than usual, and longer. She slapped at him playfully. "Don't you call me bright-eyes, you fresh thing, you!"

One of the lamps in the drugstore went out. Rose was paralyzed with fear. Mr. Coday was closing up. In a moment he would step into the street and see her, out at night, talking with a traveling man. Elsa's and Rose's characters would be ruined.

Mr. Andrews chuckled. He sang a line from a popular song: "Just because you made them goo-goo eyes!" His hand moved to chuck Elsa under the chin, but she turned her head with dignity and said, "Mr. Andrews, meet my friend, Miss Wilder."

He lifted his hat again and said he was pleased to meet her. Rose said gruffly, "How do you do?" The peril of what they were doing had stolen her senses. She wanted to run, but didn't know how to do it. Everything seemed frozen in that moment.

Then, without a word, Mr. Andrews took Elsa and Rose by the elbows, and, one on either side of him, they walked away from the square.

Behind them Rose heard the drugstore door slam, and the key turning in the lock. She knew they were far enough away now that Mr. Coday wouldn't recognize them.

"Mind if I smoke?" Mr. Andrews asked.

"Oh no, no indeed, not at all!" Elsa replied vivaciously. "I just love the smell of tobacco, it's so manly. I like the smell of a good cigar, I really do. I'm different from most girls that way, but I always say don't mind me at all, just go right ahead and smoke as if I wasn't there, because I enjoy the smell of tobacco, I really honestly do. Most girls don't feel that way about it, but I . . ."

On and on Elsa prattled, and Rose tried to see what it was she was doing to bewitch Mr. Andrews. Rose's feet had a solemn sound in her ears as they walked slowly all the way to the end of the boardwalk and slowly back again. Elsa and Mr. Andrews talked the whole way, but none of it made any sense to Rose.

"Oh, you kiddo!" Mr. Andrews often said, and Elsa retorted, "Skiddoo for you!" But she hung on his arm and laughed. "Oh, them goo-goo eyes!" Mr. Andrews said, sounding greatly pleased with himself.

All the while Mr. Andrews held Rose's arm. His hand closed warmly from time to time, as if the pressure meant something. But it couldn't mean anything, so Rose ignored it.

Now and then he drew her arm snugly closer and looked at her. He had a round, jolly face. The glow from his cigar showed little wrinkles at the corners of his eyes. His mustache

245

was a sandy color. Softly he said to Rose, "Hello."

Rose couldn't think of a reply, so each time she just answered "Hello."

Then all at once she noticed that he and Elsa were holding hands. Her arm was in his, her hand lay on his palm, and their fingers were interlaced. Rose pretended in fascinated embarrassment not to see those hands. So that was how Elsa did it! But how did she dare?

Finally, Mr. Andrews said good night. "Well, kiddos, the best of friends must part. I got to get some sleep. Got a big day tomorrow."

"Well, thank you for a very pleasant evening, Mr. Andrews," Elsa said smoothly. "And good-bye till we meet again."

Rose could never say anything like that, so she just said, "Good night."

When he was gone, Elsa squeezed Rose's arm. "Oh, Buster, isn't he wonderful?"

"He's all right, I guess," Rose said crossly. "How are we going to get back in, and what'll we do if your mother catches us?"

Elsa didn't know. She was in a reckless

mood from so many dangers passed. But Rose was worried.

They stole across the dewy grass in front of the Beaumont house, past the iron deer. The house was dark and still. Rose guessed it was ten o'clock, maybe even later. Elsa gently tried the front door. It was locked.

Then, shamelessly, she started taking off her clothes, right down to her cambric underwear. She wrapped her corsets and best dress in the silk petticoat and tossed the whole thing onto the porch roof. They were going to climb!

Rose took off only her shoes. Then they climbed the porch post, crawled through Elsa's window, and crept into her room, listening.

There was a faint stir in the house. Steps came cautiously down the hall. The doorknob uttered a tiny squeak. Rose and Elsa barely had time to leap into bed and draw the covers up to their chins. The door opened. Rose felt the whole bed shaking with the beating of her heart. She was certain anybody could hear it.

Elsa stirred and gasped. She whispered, "What's that? Buster! Buster, you awake?"

"Shhh!" Mrs. Beaumont hissed. "What time did you get in?"

"My goodness, Mama," Elsa complained. "Waking us up in the middle of the night, scaring us to death!"

"When?" Mrs. Beaumont repeated with emphasis. "When did you get in?"

"How do I know?" Elsa answered peevishly. "What would I look at the clock for, and you know you won't make Papa let me have a watch. If I only had a watch, I—"

"SHHH!" Mrs. Beaumont hissed. "You'll wake up your father." Then she left, closing the door gently.

Rose let out a long sigh of relief.

"Well, I've certainly got him going, haven't I," Elsa whispered. "He's just crazy about me. I guess you saw that. My goodness, anybody could see that much. You did see how crazy he is about me, didn't you, Buster?"

"Yes," said Rose.

Elsa stirred, making herself cozy for sleep.

"And he's such a man of the world, that's what I like about him. I always did say I was going to marry a nobby dresser. Why, just the way he wears his hat, you can see he's perfectly at home in the best society. And Buster, you know what I think? I think . . ."

Until sleep came to her, Rose listened while the thought burned into her that she was nothing but a dub. She would never be anything but a good, worthy girl. And other girls would get all the boys.

The Letters

Next Sunday, after the evening service at church, Rose hesitated a moment before walking out the door into the fresh night air. It was her practice to march with purpose, eyes downcast, through the corridor of boys and young men, afraid to meet a single gaze.

This time, she gathered her courage and walked slowly down the steps and the walk, her head held high, her eyes scanning the eager faces. They were all looking behind her, waiting for a prettier girl. But near the end of the walk, her eyes locked with the eyes of Ernie Tate. Rose smiled bashfully, and Ernie stepped forward to ask if he might walk her home.

Shyly she said yes, but not with any true pleasure. Ernie had red hair and freckles, and he was a country boy working his way through school. Rose didn't really like him, but she guessed he was the best she could do.

On the way home he didn't say "Oh, you kiddo!" He didn't say "Them goo-goo eyes." He didn't say much of anything.

Rose tried her best to imitate Elsa. She said, "Isn't it a lovely night?" and "The stars are lovely, aren't they?" and "I don't think it's going to rain, do you?"

Desperately she thrust her arm into his. Her heart thumped, the ground seemed to lurch under her feet, but she clutched his hand.

Ernie jumped. Both of them stared straight ahead, their hands clasped as though frozen that way. Neither of them said a word. Every step seemed an eternity. Rose looked down the street, and her house seemed miles away.

They would never reach it, and this awkward moment would go on forever.

But finally they did get close, and then they actually reached Rose's gate.

As soon as her hand touched the gate, she cried out, "Good night!" Ernie was already turned and ready to flee. He muttered, "Good night," and nearly sprinted down the street. Rose knew he would never ask to walk her home again.

She came into the house, slamming the front door so hard that Mama jumped up from the dining table where she had been writing a letter. Papa looked up from his newspaper with a scowl.

Rose could almost have cried to see Papa angry at her. In all her life she couldn't ever remember him being the least bit annoyed with her, and now she had made him cross. She tried to brush past them to go to her room, but Mama blocked her way.

"I declare," she said, "I've half a mind to give you a good dose of sulphur and molasses, for all you've had one this spring."

"A good dose of housework is what she needs," Papa said without humor. Then he added darkly, to Rose, "You best stop your gadding with that Beaumont girl, or you'll wish you had."

"Rose is a good girl," Mama said. "I can trust her never to do anything that'll make talk."

"Yes, Mama. Yes, Papa," Rose murmured, staring at her shoes.

She climbed into bed that night with guilt gnawing a jagged hole in her heart. In the next days she caught Mama watching her with a musing look, and unexpected glances from Papa. It alarmed her for hours. But it seemed nothing could make her give up the fascinated bitterness of watching Elsa's romance.

To Rose's amazement, Mama let her sleep over again at Elsa's on Wednesday. Again, with racing hearts, they stole out of the house and met Mr. Andrews. This time Elsa made Rose promise not to walk the whole way with them. "He's polite to you," she said. "But I guess you could see he'd like to talk to me by myself. I guess you saw that, didn't you?"

He met them even more jovially than before. Rose saw again the round, jolly face, the laughing eyes, the sandy mustache sleekly trimmed and waxed. The cigar clenched in his teeth was so masculine. His derby was jaunty, the shoulders of his coat perfectly padded, and watch charms hung from the chain looped across his checked vest. His oxblood shoes had the very latest knobby toes. He clasped Rose's arm warmly.

But Rose had promised, so halfway out the boardwalk she stopped. Mr. Andrews' clasp tightened. "What's the matter, kiddo?"

"I don't want to go any farther," she said. "You and Elsa go on. I'll just wait here."

"Well," Elsa cried with false outrage. "Well, of all things! Why, Buster Wilder, I never! Well, if that's the way you're acting, and after all I've done for you. Well, if you want to, all I've got to say is, you just can!"

"I do hope I've done nothing to offend you," Mr. Andrews said kindly.

Rose shook her head. "I just don't want to walk any farther."

"Well, we'll just turn around and go back," he suggested. In the moonlight Rose saw Elsa frown ferociously. Rose was bungling everything.

"I've got something in my shoe," Rose blurted.

There was a moment of embarrassment. Then Mr. Andrews said politely, "That's all right. Don't worry. I'll turn my back and you go right ahead and take it out. I won't look."

Elsa's voice leaped on Mr. Andrews, "Why, Mr. Andrews. Why, as if Buster could . . . the very idea! You come right away from here!"

Rose sat on the edge of the sidewalk while their slow steps and Elsa's voice drifted away into the moon-washed night. Sitting there in her loneliness, Rose realized with a shock that she might love Mr. Andrews, too. She had never known anyone like him.

But Mr. Andrews was Elsa's. She couldn't stop her from keeping him. A shudder of rage shook her body. She hated Elsa. And she admired her too. Rose would not let Mama separate her from Elsa. If she did, Rose could never again meet him.

That Sunday Elsa asked Rose her advice about writing a note to Mr. Andrews. Should she make the salutation "My dear Mr. Andrews?"

"Yes," Rose said, as sweetly as she could.

"I would think it's too . . . well, he isn't, not exactly, mine. Yet," Elsa said. So she decided to begin "Dear Friend" and end with, "Your true friend, Miss Elsa Beaumont."

She would not let Rose read the note, but after she had copied it on pink stationery, they went together to mail it. When it was time to part and go to their homes, Elsa suddenly began to cry. Rose demanded to know the reason. She had to badger Elsa and promise not to get mad. Finally Elsa confessed: She had told Mr. Andrews to send his reply to Rose.

Rose's heart skipped a beat. It was too incredible, just impossible to believe.

"You did *what*?"

"Oh, Buster, I just had to!" Elsa sobbed, backing around the corner of the post office so no one would see her. Rose had no pity for her tears. She was seething with rage and fear.

"You know Papa would never let me write to a traveling man," Elsa stumbled on. "I was scared he'd find out from Postmaster Gaskill. Oh, Papa'd be terrible! He'd just ruin my whole life. Please!"

"Just how am I to explain it?" Rose demanded.

Suddenly Elsa wasn't crying. She grabbed Rose's arm. "You get so many letters, nobody'll pay any attention if you get one more. They know you wouldn't be getting letters from a man.

"And when I'm married you'll always be my best friend, and I'll do anything for you. I'd give you my rhinestone combs right this minute, only Mama'd make a fuss. Oh, Buster, *please*!"

"All right. All *right*!" Rose said. She just wanted Elsa to stop babbling. "It's true, I get the mail most every day, because I get so many letters. But you must promise me something."

"Anything!" Elsa said anxiously. "Anything at all, Rose. Oh you're such a dear!"

"You have to let me read his letter when it comes."

"Why, of course!" Elsa cried in joy. "I'd have let you read it anyway. But, of course!"

They agreed to meet each day at the post office at the same time, in the late morning just before Rose had to help Mama get dinner.

A few days later Mr. Gaskill handed her an envelope with a picture on it of a hotel, and bordered with scrollwork. Elsa nearly squealed with pleasure when Rose showed it to her. They hurried away from the square like thieves, looking for a place to count their loot. They walked out toward the cemetery until they were far enough away that no one would notice.

They looked at the front of the envelope. The penmanship on the address was beautiful, with fine flourishes and inky downstrokes. "Miss Rose Wilder" was all Rose got a chance to read. Elsa snatched the letter from her hands.

Rose turned on her in fury. "Elsa Beaumont, you give me that!" She grabbed for it.

"I won't!" Elsa said, tucking her hand behind her.

"You will!"

"I won't do any such a thing!"

"You promised."

"I don't care!" Elsa said, sticking out her chin. "I guess I'm not going to let anybody read my very own love let—"

Rose slapped her. She couldn't have stopped herself if she'd wanted to, but she didn't anyway.

Elsa's face twisted with outrage. "I'll never speak to you again!" she cried out, holding her cheek. "As long as I live. Not a word!"

"Good," Rose said coldly. She was surprised how good that slap had felt. "I guess I'll manage it somehow." They both stalked off toward their homes.

But that same night at the Ladies' Aid ice cream social, before Rose knew what was happening, Elsa sidled up to her and slid her arm into Rose's. Rose resisted at first, but Elsa tugged her away from the crowd gathered around the long tables under the lantern-lighted trees.

"Oh Buster," Elsa murmured, "I could hardly wait to see you. Buster, I've made up my mind to something, and I wouldn't do it for everybody, but just for you because you're my very best friend and getting his letters for me and everything, and I know he likes you, too. So Buster"—she paused—"I'm going to name my oldest girl after you."

Rose jerked her arm away from Elsa's. "Are you going to let me read that letter?"

"Why, Buster!" She gazed at Rose, her fair hair shining and her brown eyes glimmering in the light of the Chinese lanterns. "Why, of

course. Why, I said you could! My goodness,
you didn't think I meant . . ." Elsa laughed.
Her hand squeezed Rose's arm fondly.

Rose sighed in exasperation. They walked
up and down, on the trodden earth by the
empty hitching posts. In the center of the
square the church ladies, in second-best
dresses and aprons, were spooning ice cream
from the freezers standing on the grass and
carrying the heaped saucers and plates of
layer cake to people waiting at the long
tables. They were all in their Sunday clothes
under the flickering lanterns.

Rose could see all the girls envying her
because she and Elsa had so much to confide
in each other that they didn't even want ice
cream. Now and then a boy sauntered near
them, pretending to be uninterested in them,
but Elsa dismissed each one by turning
brusquely away.

"We don't want to be bothered with boys,
do we, Buster?"

Rose sighed again and said weakly, "No."

If Mama had let Rose go home to stay at

the Beaumonts' that night, Rose might have read Mr. Andrew's letter. But that evening, after the social, Mama said no. She would never let Rose stay all night with Elsa again.

"I've had enough of all this fol-de-rol. I have eyes in my head. I can see the way Elsa schemes and connives. Whatever it is, I might never find out. But I don't want you involved. You'll stay here with me, until you get your senses back."

Mama said it with such determination, Rose knew there was no point to pleading. And anyway, it was a kind of relief not to be flirting anymore with danger. Besides, Rose knew Mama couldn't forbid her from talking to Elsa, or walking with her after church. Mama would have to explain it to Mrs. Beaumont, and Mama would never be that rude.

As she washed up and undressed for bed, Rose thought it was all just as well, the way things had turned out. She slept more peacefully than she had in a long while.

Sweet Revenge

Mr. Andrews kept writing his letters, so Rose and Elsa kept meeting at the post office every day before noon. In the next few weeks, Rose gave six letters to Elsa, but Rose never got to read a single one.

Elsa spoke of them, but she wouldn't give any to Rose to read, and Mama gave Rose only ten minutes to fetch the mail. So their conversations were short, and Rose mostly listened. Rose thought about throwing away any more letters she got for Elsa. But Elsa was always there waiting when Mr. Gaskill handed over the mail. Rose thought one day Elsa would finally give in and let her see them all.

One day Elsa said she had arranged with Mr. Andrews for Rose to meet another traveling man one night. But when the night came, Rose didn't have the courage to ask Mama if she could go uptown, or make up some lie. And, truth be told, she didn't really want to.

The next day outside the post office, Elsa scolded her.

"Men hate to be kept waiting," she complained. "I don't want you to think I blame you one bit, Buster. I honestly don't, not one bit. How can you help not being smart enough to get away somehow?

"But honestly, Buster, just for your own good you ought to try to be smarter. Men don't care what marks you make in school and things like that. They like a girl that's really smart, and you know in some ways you've got brains, you really have, because look what marks you make in school.

"So maybe if you'd try anyway to be a little bit smarter it wouldn't matter so much how you look, because I bet no matter how I looked, the boys would be just as crazy about me."

Then she touched the bosom of her dress, where she'd hidden her latest letter. "My heart's beating so, I can't hardly breathe. I do hope he's not mad at me because you kept him waiting!"

"But Elsa," Rose said hastily. "I'll get away, after church tomorrow night. You meet me on the church steps, and bring that letter."

"All right," she said brightly. "See you tomorrow, then."

But Elsa didn't show up. Rose found her in front of Coday's Drugs with Blanche. Blanche watched in open-mouthed surprise as Rose dragged Elsa away, right in the middle of their conversation.

"What did he say?" Rose demanded. "Where's that letter?"

"What letter?" Elsa asked, eyes wide and trying to sound perfectly innocent. Then, as if suddenly remembering some long ago petty detail, she answered herself, "Oh, that! Why my goodness, Buster, I don't know where that old letter is. I guess it's lying around some-place." She laughed lightly. "My goodness, Buster, you're awf'ly silly! Why I've just been fooling you the whole time. I don't care a bit for any old traveling man, and I never did."

"Why, Elsa—" Rose sputtered. "Why, you told me just yesterday that—"

"My goodness, are you such a boob you believe everything you hear?"

Rose knew for certain that something terri-ble had happened. But she couldn't for the life of her figure out what.

"Elsa, what was in that letter?"

"Oh, I don't know! I didn't pay much atten-tion. My goodness gracious, I get so many let-ters. But the truth is it just makes me kind of sick to read such mush. I don't think it's manly. If anybody's as gone on me as all that, why he can just go way back and sit down!

"I don't care any more about him than if he'd never been born. You know, Buster, I have very high ideals of what my Prince Charming will be like when he comes along, and—"

"You don't mean you're through with Mr. Andrews!" Rose couldn't believe it.

"Why, my goodness yes! My goodness gracious. I should say so!" Elsa cried. "I wouldn't cross the street to wipe my feet on a dozen Mr. Andrewses! The silly old mushy thing!"

Then her voice grew shrill. "Oh, he'll be trying to see me all right! But skiddoo for him! I'm just absolutely through with him; there's no three ways about that."

Rose was torn. She would never see Mr. Andrews again. But she admired Elsa with such a burning envy that if Mr. Andrews had appeared before them at that instant, Rose would have turned her back on him, too.

Over the next days Rose began to return to her old self. Elsa didn't meet her at the post office anymore, but they sneaked a visit now and then. As Rose got her senses back, Mama lowered her guard.

One Friday, almost a week later, Rose made an excuse to go uptown after supper. She met Elsa, as they'd planned, and walked together.

Rose listened without hearing to Elsa's prattle while they stepped carefully over the cracks in the wide boards. She realized that it wasn't even fun anymore that Mama didn't know she was with Elsa.

They were far out on the lonely end of the walk when they heard a man's steps behind them. They were terrified. Clutching each other, they looked over their shoulders, ready to run. It was Mr. Andrews.

Elsa gasped. She tore her hand from Rose's arm, snatched up her skirts, and fled past him without a word.

Rose stood stunned, too amazed to follow. She and Mr. Andrews stared at the receding flutter of Elsa's petticoats. The thudding of her feet grew faint, and she was gone.

"Well, I'll be switched," Mr. Andrews said. He turned to Rose and looked at her with beaming satisfaction. "Well, girlie! You're a smart kid!"

Rose realized with cold horror that she was alone with Mr. Andrews. She couldn't think why Elsa would do such a thing as desert her.

She didn't know what to do. No words came to her mind. Her legs had turned to stone.

"I wouldn't have believed it," Mr. Andrews said. "Well, girlie!" he repeated. "Well, kiddo! Here we are."

Then his arm was around Rose. His face came closer and grew larger in the dusky light. "Hello, kiddo!" he said softly.

None of it made sense, yet Rose replied feebly, "Hello." For an instant her eyes stared at the sandy mustache. Then, suddenly, she got her wits back and struggled out of his arm.

"Don't!" she gasped. "You mustn't! I didn't mean—" She fled, just as Elsa had. She ran all the way home, praying that Mama and Papa might be out so she could slip upstairs to her room unnoticed. When she got to the back gate, she saw lamplight in the dining-room window. She leaned against the fence until she had her breath again. She smoothed her skirts, patted her hair, and, as quietly and soberly as she could, let herself in the kitchen door.

She spotted Papa through the doorway to the dining room, sitting at the table. He looked at her with such piercing eyes, Rose felt he was reading her mind. Mama's stern voice called out, "Come in here, Rose. There's something we need to discuss."

All inside of Rose went quiet. Only her heart kept beating thickly.

Mama was sitting at the other end of the table. Her face was deathly still and tired-looking. In front of her lay an envelope. Rose saw, upside down, the picture of a hotel and the beautiful penmanship with its fine flourishes. Her scalp crinkled with terror.

"Postmaster Gaskill handed this to your father," Mama said evenly. "Said he thought he ought to let us know what's been going on."

Rose thought wildly that Elsa must have lied to her. She must have written him again, and this was his answer. Everything blurred. Rose crushed a fist against her mouth. The scandal, the scorn that she and Elsa must bear fell on her all at once.

"We've got to get to the bottom of this, Rose," Papa said. "Go on, Bess. Read it. Out loud."

Mama cleared her throat. She read, "Dear friend Buster . . ."

"What?" Rose cried, her voice strangling in her throat.

Mama repeated,

"Dear friend Buster,
Well here I am in Evansville and no answer from you. I guess maybe you thought I was too fresh to write to you the way I did. Can only say I have always been a gentleman in every respect and would for no consideration hurt a sweet little girl's feelings. Can only say no disrespect was intended and I hope none taken. Well, little girl, I am still thinking of your big blue eyes and will try to make your town on the freight Friday. If so will stroll out on the board-walk about five o'clock hoping you will do the same and would kindly appreciate you bringing some other friend that will not talk too much, ha ha. Well will say no more at this time, so no more till I see your big beautiful eyes.
                from Yrs. Respectfully,
                A.B. Andrews (Andy)."

Rose was sobbing when Mama finished. "You leave this to me, Manly," Mama said. "Let's only hope it's no worse."

"Worse!" Papa thundered. "For all we know, the whole town's talking. How long has this been going on? What does he mean, 'some other friend that will not talk too much'? What's this they want hushed up? Who's been talking?"

Rose couldn't stop crying. "You leave this to me, Manly," Mama repeated.

Mama put Rose to bed and sat on the edge while Rose told everything, except that Mr. Andrews almost kissed her. She couldn't tell Mama that.

Once, in the middle of her story, Mama said grimly, "I feel it my duty to take this up with Mrs. Beaumont."

When Rose had finished, Mama was silent awhile, staring into her lap. Then she patted Rose's shoulder and stood up.

"You girls nowadays think you're altogether too smart," she said. "I must say I don't know what the world's coming to. Disobedience, disrespect, lying, sneaking, running in the streets at all hours.

"You might know what it would end in. Meeting strange men! It's only the mercy of God it hasn't got out and ruined your character for good and all. If folks did find out, Rose, you know as well as I do, you'd never be able to hold your head up again."

Rose shivered just thinking about it.

"But I see you know you've done wrong, and repent it. Let it be a lesson to you."

Then she blew out the lamp. "Now try to get some sleep, and you'll feel better in the morning."

"Mama," Rose piped up.

"Yes," Mama answered as she began to back down the ladder. She stood, half of her hidden by the hole in the floor, the light from below making a halo of her hair.

"What about Papa?" Rose whispered. "I never saw him so . . . so . . ." Then Rose lost her voice again to tears of shame and remorse.

"Don't you worry about Papa," said Mama. "I'll fix it with him. Now get some sleep."

Rose felt better already. The thought of Elsa reading that mushy letter was sweet revenge. Mr. Andrews had written it for Rose, and now Elsa would know that Rose knew he had written it to her. Now Rose knew why that other letter had made Elsa so mad, why it ended her love for Mr. Andrews. Rose wondered what he had written. But she never wanted to see him again.

And then Rose savored another thought. She hadn't let Mr. Andrews kiss her. She had saved her first kiss for the man who would be her husband. That was something, anyway, a kind of triumph.

She saw clearly, for the first time in her life, that no one could make her be good anymore. She was too old for that. Her teachers, Reverend Mays, even Mama and Papa—none of them could make her be worthy, or any of the things Rose knew made a person wholesome and noble. She had to be that person by herself, now. And she knew, to the tips of her toes, that she would.

Best of all, Rose no longer had the slightest

fear that she would end up an old maid. As sleep overtook her, she promised herself to write a nice long letter to Paul. She wanted to tell him how much she had come to admire the new president, Teddy Roosevelt, and to ask if he liked him, too.

Just a Woman of the House

Rose never did have to bow her head in public shame. No one who knew what had happened breathed a word of it. But she could have borne any amount of scandal before she could bear another moment of Papa's disapproval. When he told her the next morning that the whole affair was forgotten, and hugged her warmly, Rose couldn't stifle a small sob of relief.

"There, there," Papa said in a husky voice. "You can't blame your old father for wanting the best for his girl. Now let's just get on with it. I see the woodbox is almost empty."

Mama went to see Mrs. Beaumont and came back with a satisfied look on her face. Rose, too, had to admit she'd have liked to gloat a bit over Elsa's foolishness and lies. She would have liked to give that girl a dose of her own bitter medicine.

But she wanted nothing more to do with her. Ever. She never wanted to hear another word of her vain and empty woolgathering. The first time she saw Elsa coming toward her on the street, Rose ducked into Reynolds' and waited for her to pass.

The only person who ever asked about it was Blanche. Now that she was home for the summer from Mountain Grove Academy, she and Rose began to pass their time together again. Rose had gone to Prairie Hollow Church with Blanche one Sunday. The Beaumonts' fancy buggy drove past them on the street, with Mr. and Mrs. Beaumont and Elsa's four sisters. Elsa had not shown her face in church for a month of Sundays.

"Whatever happened between you and Elsa?" Blanche asked. "All that whispering and carrying on. And Maude Reynolds said you two had an awful fight of some kind."

"It was nothing, really," Rose answered. A faint flush of remembered shame dampened her temples.

"Oh, come on, Rose, you can tell me," Blanche pressed. "After all, we are the best of friends."

"To get a friend, close one eye. To keep her, close both," Rose said coyly. "Maybe some day. But I can't say now. So don't bother asking again."

Blanche chuckled. "Well, you just better tell me one day. I won't be satisfied with some old proverb."

Rose asked Blanche a thousand questions about Mountain Grove. What did the school look like? What were the lessons? Did she like her teacher? The other scholars? And everything Blanche told Rose made her want more than ever to go there.

"The school is very large," said Blanche. "Two whole stories, with so many windows and classrooms—twelve in all. It sits in a beautiful park of tall shady trees, and there are benches. It's a wonderfully peaceful place to sit and read in nice weather.

"Of course, most of the rooms are for the lower grades. The academy is really just one large class. There were nineteen academy scholars this year, from everywhere in southern Missouri. And only the best students can go."

"What is the teacher like?" Rose wanted to know. "Is it a woman or a man?"

"Oh, it's a man. I didn't think I would like another man for a teacher, but Professor Lynch is just wonderful. He almost never sits. He's always moving around the room in a quick and lively way. But it doesn't make anyone nervous because he has such a kind and good-humored voice. I could listen to him for hours and never tire of it. There isn't a stuffy, boresome bone in his body, I think.

"And he is very polite with us scholars. He's always finding something about a person to compliment and never scolds.

"He has so many interesting things in the room. A tellurion, a planetarium, a piano just for our class, and so many books."

"What in the world is a tellurion, and that other thing?"

"A tellurion is a kind of machine that shows the daily rotation of the earth, and the annual revolution. And a planetarium is a model of the planetary system. I adore learning about the heavens. Just think, there are scientists who believe there might actually be life on other planets. Can you imagine?"

Rose's head was spinning.

"Professor Lynch takes us all outside on the clearest nights, to study the constellations and find the planets. In the best weather he gives the lesson outside. He makes it into a picnic. We have gatherings at his house with Mrs. Lynch, who is so interesting and gracious. She has even been to Egypt!"

"Do you like the other scholars?"

"Oh yes," Blanche said. "We are like a big family, because almost everyone is boarding away from their homes. We do just everything together, and have such a good time. We had three dances this year, and more socials at the Lynchs' than I could count. Of course, I missed some of them because I came home on the weekends. It just seems we're always laughing.

"And," Blanche said, lowering her voice, "there is a boy who likes me, from West Plains. His name is Arthur Raney, and he has curly brown hair and the most beautiful speckled-green eyes. He's very sweet and kind. He brings me wildflowers, and he wrote a poem for me, too."

Rose fought back a wave of envy.

"Blanche Coday," Rose said breathlessly. "Did he kiss you? Are you in love?"

"Oh, no!" Blanche cried out. "Heavens no! He's very proper, a perfect gentleman. But we do hold hands now and then. In love? I hardly think I could be. I might never. No, I'm going to wait for the right man, and I'm going to get to know him as well as my own self before I say yes to marriage.

"That's what Mrs. Lynch tells us: 'Marry in

haste, repent at leisure.' I want to have a marriage as perfect as Professor and Mrs. Lynch's. Why, they've been married twenty years, and to see them together you would think for all the world that they had just started courting. No, I'm going to take my sweet time about that.

"After all, Rose, it's a whole life of living. And girls are getting married later and later, now. It's no shame at all to wait and see."

Rose was awestruck by Blanche. She seemed completely changed. She had been a little bit like Elsa before she went to the academy. Not boy-crazy, or vain, but in other small ways that Rose thought rich girls were the same. Rich girls didn't worry much about their futures, or stare longingly at the latest fabrics and fashions in store windows, or take much of an interest in the changing world beyond the edge of town.

Now the new way Blanche walked, the way she spoke, she seemed so full of confidence and poise and purpose. Living away from home, going to the academy, had grown her right up. Blanche was becoming a woman of the world, while Rose was still just a woman of the house, chained to a life of drudgery.

Mountain Grove sounded like paradise, just the place for her. And the school was only twenty miles east, two stops on the local train. "If only there were a way. If only there were *some* way!"

"Well, there just might be," said Blanche.

"How?" Rose demanded. "What do you mean?"

"Some of the students at the academy are given scholarships," Blanche explained. "I don't know if you could have one. You would have to ask and see."

"What's a scholarship?"

"Well," Blanche began awkwardly. "Well, it's a way for . . . for people who can't pay the cost to still attend."

"But who pays, if they can't? Where does the money come from?"

"From people who give it," said Blanche. "They give it to Professor Lynch, and he gives it to the students he thinks deserve it."

"Oh," Rose said, nodding her head slowly. "Oh. It's charity, isn't it? For poor people."

"Oh, Rose, it's not like that!" Blanche protested. "I hope you don't . . . you mustn't think like that. Those students, they're just the same as everyone else. Professor Lynch believes everyone should have an equal chance for a first-rate education. That's why he gives the scholarships."

Rose really didn't care how she might have the chance to go to Mountain Grove Academy. But she knew what Mama would say if charity were involved. And she was always needed at home. Still, Rose had to ask. She waited for a quiet supper, on a night when they had no boarders and Mama and Papa seemed to be in a good mood.

Rose was nervous, and full of dread. It took her until the pie was served to build up her courage. She began by telling them all that Blanche had said about the academy, except the cost.

"Professor Lynch sounds like a wonderful teacher," Mama said, pouring three cups of coffee, and passing one to Papa and the other to Rose.

"Mama," Rose rushed on, "I'll be graduating from school next year. But Blanche said I'm so far ahead in my lessons that even this year . . . well, I wish more than anything in the world that I could go to Mountain Grove with her," she declared. She sank back in her chair and blew out her cheeks, as winded as if she had just run a foot race.

Mama took a sip of her coffee and set the cup down carefully in its saucer. She glanced at Papa for a moment.

"I guess I know when there's a game of cat and mouse being played," Mama said. "All right, Rose. How much?"

Rose gulped. "Well, Blanche said her father pays about . . . about twenty dollars. But that's room and board as well as tuition," she added quickly.

"Twenty dollars for a whole year?" Papa asked. "Why, that's not—"

"No, Papa. It's for a month."

"A month!" Papa chortled. "Phew! Imagine

that, Bess. That's near seven barrels of number one apples, every month. Tarnation!"

"Rose, you know as well as we do that—what is it, a hundred and eighty dollars a year?—is just impossible."

"But Mama, there might be a way," Rose said.

Mama raised an eyebrow and leaned forward.

"Well, Blanche says that Professor Lynch gives scholarships to deserving students. Only the brightest and the best students, from good homes. It's not charity or anything, because Professor Lynch says—"

"How can a person get such a scholarship?" Mama asked, her eyes brightening.

Rose's heart skipped a beat. She was so shocked to see Mama's interest that she stammered, "I . . . Blanche said . . . well, I don't know, exactly. She said you have to ask and see."

"Sounds like a long shot to me," Papa said.

Rose's spirits dipped.

"Maybe so," Mama answered thoughtfully. "If Rose were just an average student, I should say it might not be worth the trying. But she's beyond the ninth grade in her lessons. Far beyond. She's read practically every one of Mrs. Rippee's books. And you know yourself, Manly, that women today are moving ahead in almost every field. Why shouldn't our daughter have the same chance as the next girl to improve herself?"

Papa nodded agreement.

"Oh, Mama, really?"

"We'll write to this Professor Lynch, and see what can be done for it. Now don't go hanging all your hopes on this, Rose. I have no doubt you would be found suitable as a student. But we only have Blanche's word that such a scholarship even exists."

But Rose hung her hopes on it anyway. She simply had to. There was nothing else for her to look forward to.

Mama wrote a letter to Professor Lynch. She read it aloud to Rose before she posted it.

"*Dear Professor Lynch,*

*Please forgive us for imposing on you
in this manner, but my husband, Mr. A. J.
Wilder, and I would like to inquire after the
possibility of our daughter, Rose, attending
Mountain Grove Academy.*

*We have learned from one of your students,
Miss Blanche Coday, of the fine work you
are doing with your students. If we may be
permitted to boast just a bit, Rose is an
exemplary student. She has surpassed all
the other students in our local school and is
an enthusiastic reader on her own. She has
read many of the classic works of literature,
reads the newspapers, and is a quick study
on nearly any topic, although she is not so
fond of mathematics.*

*Long ago, before I was married, I taught
school myself, in South Dakota. I have spent
many hours giving Rose some of her lessons
at home and have endeavored to instill in
her a love of knowledge, as well as a desire
to develop a pure, upright character.*

We are wondering what might be done

*to advance her studies, as our school only
teaches to the ninth grade. I have no doubt
that you would find her a suitable candidate.*

*However, there is a difficulty in that we
are somewhat limited in our resources at
this time. We are farmers, and every cent we
have is spoken for in meeting our essential
obligations.*

*Miss Coday has told Rose that there may
be the possibility of a grant or scholarship to
assist worthy students to attend Mountain
Grove Academy. We would be grateful for
any encouragement you might be able to give
us in this regard.*

We await the favor of your reply.

Very truly yours,
Mrs. A.J. Wilder"

Mama folded the letter, put it in an envelope, and gave it to Rose to take to the post office. She was too old to skip, and anyway her long skirts would have tangled and gotten muddy if she'd tried. But her heart soared and her head swam with visions of socials and picnic lessons and, most of all, escape from her everyday life.

She watched Postmaster Gaskill put on the stamp, and lingered until she saw him drop the envelope in the mailbag. She crossed her fingers and said a silent prayer: Please, please, let my dream come true!

Each morning for the next three days, Rose raced to the post office, trembling with hope that she would find a letter from Professor Lynch. Each day she walked soberly home, empty-handed, to help Mama prepare dinner.

"You must learn a bit of patience," Mama chided as Rose moped through her chores. "School is out for the summer. Perhaps he is traveling. There could be a hundred reasons why he doesn't answer as quickly as you might want."

One day, just as they were sitting down to dinner, there was a knock on the front door. Rose answered it, and found Luther Morton, the boy who had taken Paul Cooley's job at the depot.

"I got a wire for Mrs. Wilder," he said, taking off his cap.

In her excitement, Rose almost shrieked. "Mama!" she shouted. "It's a wire for you. Hurry!"

Rose was nearly jumping out of her skin by the time Mama had found a nickel, given it to Luther, and taken the envelope.

"Want me to wait for a reply, ma'am?" Luther asked.

"No, thank you," said Mama. She closed the door, tore open the envelope, unfolded the thin yellow paper, and read it to herself.

Rose's stomach churned as she studied Mama's face. It went still, like a mask, as if someone had just clicked off a light. Then her face crumpled. A choked-off sob escaped her throat. A hand flew to her mouth, and she dropped the telegram.

A chill raced down Rose's spine, and her heart seemed to stop in her breast. She picked up the telegram, her hand shaking, and read:

291

PA DEATHLY ILL STOP ASKS FOR YOU
STOP CAN YOU COME HOME STOP
SIGNED CARRIE INGALLS

Mama choked back another sob.

"Run and catch Luther!" she said. "Hurry!"

Rose dashed out the door, down the walk, and through the gate. Luther was crouched in the street, petting the Gaskills' dog.

"Luther!" Rose shouted desperately, her voice catching. "Come back!"

When he and Rose came into the parlor, Mama's cheeks were wet, but she had gained her composure. Papa sat next to her on the tête-à-tête in the parlor, holding her hand, while Luther wrote down Mama's reply on his pad:

TELL PA AM COMING SOONEST
TRAIN STOP WILL WIRE ARRIVAL
TIME STOP

Rose could hardly believe her ears. Everything had happened so fast. Grandpa Ingalls was dying. And after eight long years, Mama was going all the way back to South Dakota to see him. It was too incredible to imagine.

"How do you want to sign it, Mrs. Wilder?" Luther asked shyly.

"'Laura,'" said Mama, dabbing her eyes with her handkerchief. "Just sign it 'Laura.'"

The Longest Mile

Mama woke with a start in the dimly lit railway passenger carriage. She rubbed her neck to soothe a painful crick she'd gotten from sleeping sitting up. Her mind was fuzzy from two days without proper rest, and an odd dream she'd just been having, about being caught in a spider's web. No, she had been crawling across a spider's web.

Then she chuckled to herself. She *was* in a spider's web, the web of steel rails that crisscrossed the country, the web of rails that was bringing her home to De Smet.

The seats around her were empty. Only

four other people sat in the car. The turned-down lanterns jiggled and swung from their hooks in the ceiling, casting murky, swooping shadows.

Mama was nearing the last leg of her long journey home to see her pa. She had been riding a local train through the middle of the night across the flat, treeless prairies. She looked out the window at the dark land, but the moon had already set. Her reflection looked back at her, eyes puffy, her lace collar askew, and her hair a bit matted. Mama tucked a stray strand back in place. It was hard to stay tidy riding on a train.

She sat back in her seat as a knot gathered itself in the pit of her stomach. Please let Pa be alive when I get there, she prayed. Please don't let him die before I can see him one last time. Memories of her childhood flooded her mind like glimpses of long-forgotten dreams.

In fact, the whole trip had felt like a dream. Everything had happened so fast, it hardly seemed real. She'd left Mansfield in the middle of the night, catching Number 206 at 3:05

in the morning. She hadn't slept before she left, her mind was so addled by worry and planning.

As soon as she had the wire from Carrie, she'd sent Rose to Mrs. Helfinstine, to borrow a grip. She'd sent Almanzo to the depot to see about her ticket. It was a terrible expense, forty-two dollars they could hardly spare. But it would have been unthinkable to refuse Pa. He had never asked her to come home before, so she knew it was important. She was only sorry she hadn't done it earlier, before Pa got so sick.

Mama remembered how frantic it had been, getting packed to leave. But Rose had been wonderfully helpful, ironing her dresses and shirtwaists without a peep. And Rose had made supper for her and Almanzo as well.

Mama thought of Rose with a tinge of pity and regret. She was proud of how her daughter was turning out, smarter than she or Almanzo ever were. How she wished Professor Lynch could make it possible for Rose to further her studies. As hard as it would be to do without her at home, Mama knew Rose needed to be among young people who were more of her mind.

Rose was a good, responsible girl, in spite of her independent nature. Mama had tried to be a good mother, strict but not too smothering. She understood how lonely it must have been for Rose all those years growing up without a brother or a sister. Mama still cherished the memories of the time she had spent with her three sisters. And Rose had so many more chores than Mama had as a girl, when there were many hands to divide up the work.

As Rose had started to become a young lady, Mama had tried to be more patient. She'd seen how Rose had admired Elsa. Even though Mama hated for Rose to fall under the influence of girls like her, she had decided to let Rose discover for herself that Elsa was not a true friend.

But as mature as Rose could be, she had some things to learn about people and life. Mama still shuddered to think about the traveling man.

The pity was that Mama had left Rose, only fifteen years old, as the woman of the house. Rose would have to do all of Mama's chores, as well as her own, until Mama got back. Who knew how long she might be away, and it being spring with the garden needing to be weeded. Out on the farm the spring chores were piling up, and the corn needed to be hoed.

Then there was the housework, the washing, the baking, and always, every day, the chickens to be pampered so they would keep laying. Mama reminded herself to write to Rose about not giving the chickens too much mash if the weather turned extra hot.

Oh well, Mama thought. There was no loss without some small gain. For the first time in many, many years, she had no chores to do. She could only sit on the jolting train and watch the countryside hurrying past.

Mama was simply amazed at how the country had changed in the eight years since she and Almanzo and Rose emigrated in covered wagons with the Cooleys from South Dakota to Missouri. They had camped along the way, and it had taken them six weeks to make the six-hundred-mile journey to Mansfield.

Now, in less than two days, she would be home. The railroads had conquered the whole West. It wasn't even called the West anymore, as it had been when Mama was a little girl. It was the Middle West now. The true West was California.

Coming into Kansas City she had peered out the dust-streaked windows at crowded neighborhoods of ramshackle gray houses and streets. It had been morning, and hordes of men hurried off to work, just like the cattle she saw being driven to slaughter in the huge stockyards.

She had been shocked at the sprawling, soot-stained factories and packing houses that had sprung up all along the tracks, belching clouds of foul-smelling smoke from their tall stacks. She had to cover her mouth and nose with her handkerchief, the air there was so horrid.

She had chatted for a time with a young

couple sitting across the aisle from her. They were from Ash Grove, Missouri, on their way to Chicago to start a new life. They were married only a year and had decided to give up farming his father's land.

"We want to get ourselves ahead a little," the young man had said, leaning forward, his eyes eager and full of hope. "It was hard on Papa. He always figured on me staying and taking over the place, and watching his grandchildren growing up. But it's all new times now. Why, a fellow can get two dollars a day, week in and week out, doing factory work. And a foreman makes three times as much.

"Living in the cities is a cinch against farming. The water comes right into your kitchen, and the milk's delivered right to your door. I'll be blamed if I'll let my Alice wear herself out slaving for chickens and pigs and cows." He'd taken his pretty young wife's hand and looked at her lovingly. She had smiled and blushed.

"I'm aiming to get what I can out of life," he'd declared. "Money's what makes the mare go."

Mama listened politely, but hearing the young man talk so made her feel very old. Her mind wandered as she gazed out the window at the engine smoke trailing away across the fields like a writhing snake.

When Mama was a young bride-to-be she had begged Almanzo to give up farming. She didn't want to be always poor, working hard while the merchants in the towns took it easy and made money off the farmers' backs.

But Almanzo had persuaded her that farmers were the only folks who had their freedom. The merchants needed the farmer or they had no trade. But a farmer didn't need the merchants. A farmer was his own boss.

Seventeen years had passed since then. They had sixty acres of land, mortgaged to the bank, of course, and the house in town. They expected a good harvest from the orchard this fall, but who could tell? One disaster could wipe them out. And Almanzo wasn't truly his own boss. He had to work for Mr. Waters, and run his draywagon, to make the ends meet.

Seventeen years of backbreaking work and heartache and disappointment, and still they didn't know from one year to the next if they would make it.

The young man had a point, Mama knew. But she knew something else, too: the grass is always greener on the other side of the fence. City living was no paradise. As well as she had been able to make out from the newspapers, something like a war was going on in the cities. A flood of immigration was bringing thousands of Europe's poorest people to America. The streets were hardly safe to walk at night, and hogs had more space to roam around.

The young men who were fleeing the farms found work in hot, grimy factories making plow blades or bicycles or salt pork, or any of the thousand different things that a machine could make now instead of a person's hands.

Those factories and slaughterhouses were horribly filthy and dangerous, and the men who worked in them slaved eight and more hours a day just to feed their families and pay rent to live in another man's house. They had to pay cash money for every mouthful of food. They could never get ahead, or own a scrap of land to call their own. They were good as slaves. No wonder there had been strikes, and riots, and even killings as the factory workers fought the owners for better wages and conditions. Mama pitied those men, condemned to do that same thing every day forever.

But she wondered that they were letting this happen to them. If factory work was so unbearable it made you want to kill another soul, or give up your own life, why would anyone keep at it? Farmers everywhere in the country were crying out for strong, willing pairs of hands to help keep up the farms. It wasn't an easy life, farming. But it didn't make you want to kill anyone.

Mama was a Populist, just as her pa was. She believed that every person in America was important, not just the big men who ran the country and the trusts. It was the common people who had built America. They had to

fight, one person at a time, to win their freedom, against nature as well as against King
George.

But a common person fighting for freedom
was not just a leaf, floating aimlessly down
the river. Mama couldn't help thinking of all
the dangers Pa and the rest of her family
faced when she was growing up: fire, blizzards, wolves—the list was endless. They
almost died so many times over that she had
long ago lost count. There had been no one to
complain to, or demand help from. They survived on their own, with hard work, providence, and wonderful neighbors.

She and Almanzo had moved to Missouri
because they couldn't survive another year on
the burned-out prairie. It didn't make any
sense to stay in a place where life was unliv-
able.

She still pitied those young men in their
factories, but she pitied the whole world, too.
The new times seemed like a huge, unknow-
able beast that was swallowing up the old way
of life. Everyone talked of getting ahead, of

making money. Everyone dreamed of getting rich. Yet there seemed to be less hope and happiness than she remembered folks' having when she was a child.

Mama felt a wave of gratitude toward Almanzo for convincing her to keep at farming. A farmer might never get rich, but at least he didn't have to depend on anyone else for food and shelter. To Mama's way of thinking, that was true freedom.

When the train reached Kansas City and they parted, Mama had told the young couple, "I wish you all the joy in the world." But she doubted they would find it in Chicago.

In Kansas City she'd had to change trains and wait in the depot for her connection. The inside, huge and hollow, was made of marble and polished oak. The high arches that held up the high ceiling were decorated with enormous sculptures of women and men in loose robes. Crowds of hurrying people, of every possible description, pushed and shoved their way through the doors like columns of determined ants.

It was a relief when her connecting train left, heading north toward Omaha through Iowa. The landscape in Iowa had been so restful to look at, with its seas of tender green corn shoots, its shimmering fields of barley on the right, and the Big Muddy, the Missouri River, on the left.

In Omaha that evening the train had passed more factories, stockyards, and slaughterhouses, and she made another change of trains. As fast as the trains could go—she heard the conductor say up to sixty miles an hour—Mama felt she could not get home fast enough. If she had been with Almanzo, she might have taken a room in Omaha for the night, to rest up. But she was alone, and anyway there wasn't a moment to spare.

As the train flung her forward in space, she flew backward through time, crossing almost thirty-five years of her life, back to when she was a little girl. It seemed like yesterday that they had emigrated to Missouri, like last week when she had married Almanzo, and only a year or two since she was a little girl, helping her ma with the chores in the little house on the prairie, or nearly drowning in Plum Creek, or watching Pa make his bullets in the Big Woods of Wisconsin.

Somewhere out there in the vast stretches of the vast country sliding past her eyes were all the memories of her youth. Those were memories not just of her own time gone by, but time gone by for all of America. The frontier was closed, the Indians banished to their reservations, and every corner of the country settled up.

No one born today would ever believe the incredible things she and her family had seen. She meant to write it all down someday, for Rose's children to read when she was gone to her own reward. But just living took up all her time. It would have to wait until she was older.

The sun was setting as the train had pulled out of Omaha heading northwest toward Sioux Falls. Mama had been sorry to see darkness cloak the land. She had wanted to bring her Bible, but it was too big and heavy. She had read all the newspapers she could find that had been left on the seats by other passengers. So she just sat and thought and remembered.

Finally, she took off her hat, put her handkerchief over the seat back, and closed her eyes. She slept in feverish fits and starts, awakening every time the car rattled or banged, or the train rumbled across a trestle or roared through a tunnel. She woke every time it pulled into one of the countless little depots and milk stops along the way. In the larger towns she would look out the window and see in the dim lantern light the hurrying porters, passengers waiting to board, hacks, a freight wagon, and a sign. Then the train lurched forward again, plunging through the darkness.

At the milk stops it was just a lone farmer with his wagon, the only person awake for miles and miles around. The train barely stopped long enough for him to load his butter and eggs and milk into the baggage car.

It was something to imagine that all across

the country the same thing was happening in a hundred other small towns. The railroads had become the veins of America, rivers of life flowing to and from every nook and cranny. The covered wagon had become a relic of the past.

When she woke up to find a faint haze of light in the eastern sky, Mama came wide awake and could not sleep any longer. They were in South Dakota now. She strained her eyes to see if the land looked as she had remembered it.

The first thing she could see was that the hedges had grown higher. As the light grew, she noticed that the farms were larger, too. In the middle of fields closed in by barbed wire, she could see the ghostly shapes of abandoned homestead shanties, with cows grazing in the tall grasses around them.

Here and there the first rays of pink-and-gold light showed a lived-in house, graceless as a paperboard box, looking as if it had been just dropped on the treeless plains. Barbed wire fences ran everywhere at right angles.

The towns looked slapped together, piles of flimsy wooden sheds with painted pine battlements.

But one thing hadn't changed. The wind was blowing, as it always had, tousling the stands of young wheat like babies' hair. As the first slice of sun peeked over the edge of the earth, and lit the tips of the grassy wheat like candles, Mama felt a surge of energy course through her body. A painful stab of love and loss ached in her soul.

She remembered how each spring when Pa's tender wheat sprouted, new hope sprang in their chests. That hope became almost painful by the time the tall wheat nodded and swirled in the winds of July. Day after day, Pa would get the family together after supper, and they would snatch a few moments to go to look at it.

"Isn't it grand?" Pa would shout in his big hearty voice. And they would all say yes, and admire the heavy-headed field, big as a lake, rippling like gold cloth, whispering to them of plenty and comfort.

Mama remembered how hard they worked at harvest time, from lamplight to moonlight, their clothes sopping with sweat and filled with stickers, arms aching, fingers raw and chafed, backs crying out against the heavy bundles.

She remembered how hard Ma and she and her sisters worked cooking for the threshers, washing and ironing, milking the cows, churning the butter, feeding the horses and watering them while Pa kept at the shocking.

And she remembered all the forces that came against them: grasshoppers, wind, hail, the bitter winters, and the hot, dry summers. The prairie had drawn Pa and thousands of other men with the promise of free land and independence. But nothing good ever came without hardship and sacrifice, and Pa had had more than his share.

All of this Mama saw in her mind's eye as she gazed out the window. The rising sun became so bright it swallowed up the houses and fences and windmills, and she had to squint against the brilliance. All she could see was the prairie, the lovely enormous golden meadow that stretched far away in every direction, to the very edge of the world.

In a few hours more she would be with her family again. She had come a long way and was anxious to finish her journey. But the longest mile is the last mile home. So she sat back and rested her eyes.

Good-bye

Mama could not stop her tears of joy as she rode in the hack on the short ride home to Ma and Pa's house. She wouldn't let go of Mary's hand, and could barely speak for fear a sob would come out instead of words. Carrie had come out with Mary to meet her at the depot. Ma and Grace had stayed home with Pa.

Pa was alive! Mama kept saying it over and over again to herself. Pa was alive! And in a few minutes she would see him again.

"In fact, he has improved some," Mary said. "Although I feel to warn you, Laura, Ma says he is much changed." Mama had noticed at the depot that Mary's face had changed, too. It had a little crookedness to it now. Mama remembered that Pa had taken her to Minneapolis to have her neuralgia treated. The doctor had cut some of the most painful nerves in her face, which caused some of her muscles to relax a bit.

"Yes, Pa knows you're coming, Laura. He even smiled when we told him. He's still very weak, but he can see and hear and speak." Then Mary squeezed Mama's hand as her blind eyes looked straight ahead. Mary blinked, and a tear rolled down her cheek. "Oh, Laura, it's so good to have you home again. I have so missed your voice. And at a time such as this, you can't imagine."

"I have missed you, too. All of you," Mama said softly. "It has been too long."

Although she was bone tired, Mama's eyes eagerly scanned the buildings along Main Street, the merchants and other businesses, and Pa's old store. Nothing much had changed, she was surprised to see, except that the town looked a bit more prosperous than she remembered. It was spring, and many of the storefronts sported fresh coats of paint, and new roofs. The boardwalks had been extended too.

"Oh, look," Mama cried out. "Mr. Boast has a real estate office now."

"Yes," Mary said. "He moved off the farm when Ellie's rheumatism got so bad. I wrote you of it. He is very prosperous at it, too. I think he has something of a Midas touch, the way he can make things grow. He even got Ellie a hired girl."

"Things in town have improved some since you left," said Carrie. "More folks are coming west to try their luck at farming. And the crops have been better, although everyone still complains of the low prices.

"Look, there is Mr. Sherwood, coming out of the *De Smet News* office with his little boy, Aubrey. Mr. Sherwood is wearing that new vest I told you about, Mary. The one with the bright red pattern. Aubrey's making a face, and Mr. Sherwood is having to drag him along."

Mama smiled to herself. When Mary had first gone blind, Mama had been her eyes, telling her everything she saw. Now Carrie had become Mary's eyes.

"Can you even remember when there was no town here?" Mama asked her sisters. "When there was nothing but grass and sky, and the lakes?"

"I remember," Mary said quickly.

"I remember, too," said Carrie. "I remember the surveyors' house we lived in that winter, and the building of the railroad. Mr. Sherwood had me write some articles for the newspaper, about the founding of the town. Pa helped me with it."

Finally the driver turned the team onto Third Street and brought the hack to a halt in front of the house. The row of poplar trees along the curb had grown so tall, casting deep, restful shadows on the front lawn and roof. Next door, in the vacant lot Pa owned, the garden had been turned and planted. Two rows of young peas were the only thing that had sprouted. The two-story house looked so clean and tidy, with Mary's rocking chair on the little porch.

The front door opened, and Ma stepped onto the threshold. She looked like a little doll of an old lady, with her white hair and hands clasped in front of her. It was all Mama could do to keep herself from jumping off the hack and running to her. But when the driver had helped her down, she hurried up the walk and fell into Ma's open arms.

"Oh, Ma!" Mama sobbed. Ma felt so good, soft and still warm from the cookstove. She smelled of yeast and spices. Mama felt like a little girl. "I've missed you so."

"We have missed you, too, Laura," Ma said with a sad smile. "There, there. You must be tired from your long journey. You mustn't let yourself go on so. It wouldn't be good for Pa."

"Yes, Ma," Mama said, drying her cheeks with her handkerchief. She wondered if her eyes would ever be dry again.

"Now come with me," Ma said gently. "I

woke him up when I heard the train whistle. He's very tired, but he wants to see you."

Mama followed Ma into the dark parlor while the driver brought up her grip. Everything looked just as she remembered it. There was Ma's whatnot that Pa had made for her one Christmas. On it was the china shepherdess that had somehow miraculously survived all through the years.

Ma's rocking chair that Pa had made for her sat in the corner. The antimacassars that Mama had knitted for Ma one year still lay on the settee. But best of all, the house smelled of home and comfort and family. Mama's heart filled to bursting.

She followed Ma into the even darker bedroom. It took a moment for her eyes to adjust. Then she saw the bed, with Pa's head sticking out from the covers. His arms were on top of the quilt, and his enormous gray beard lay between them. His eyes were closed. His wrinkled cheeks were hollow, and his eyes seemed to be set so deep. He looked very, very old.

Mama fought to keep from showing her surprise to Ma. Her legs seemed unsteady, and she hesitated in the doorway, unsure what to do. Ma stood at the foot of the bed for a quiet moment. Then Pa opened his eyes, looked at Ma, then at Mama, and cracked a thin smile.

"Well, well," his weak, rasping voice called out to her. The words came slowly, with little pauses. "How's my . . . little half-pint . . . o' cider half drunk up?"

Suddenly Mama found her strength and crossed the rag carpet. She lowered herself into the chair next to his bed, and reached out to touch his fragile, bony hand. Pa slowly turned his hand palm up, so Laura could hold it. The skin was cool to the touch, and papery thin. But it was Pa's hand, his living, feeling hand. Mama felt her fears and worries melting away. She knew she wouldn't cry.

She leaned forward and looked him in the eyes. "Hello, Pa," she said softly. As she looked at him, she made herself see the Pa she knew when she was young and he was her strong and cheerful father. Even though Pa's body was old and worn out, she could see a twitch at the corners of his eyes, and a twinkle in them, that was the Pa she remembered.

"I guess you can see how I am, Pa," Mama said. "I'm an old married woman now, a whole gallon of cider that no one has even sipped."

Pa's face slowly crumpled into a true smile. He coughed once. It was as close to a laugh as he could come.

"You look well fed . . . and pretty as ever."

"Thank you, Pa. It's so good to see you again. I have missed everyone so much. But now I'm here, and we are all together again."

Pa nodded and squeezed Mama's hand.

He closed his eyes for a long moment, took a breath and then opened them again. "It's a comfort to have you here. I know it was a great trouble."

"No, Pa," Mama said quickly. "You mustn't think that. I should have come before."

Pa squeezed Mama's hand again.

"Charles," Ma said. Pa turned his head to

look at her. "Charles, I think you should let yourself rest some more. Laura will be here, and there will be plenty of time for visiting."

She fussed with his bedclothes while Mama leaned forward and placed a feathery kiss on Pa's forehead. Then she and Ma left the room, closing the door quietly behind them.

"He just had his morphine," Ma said. "It makes him very sleepy. He will be more himself when he wakes up. Now come with me into the kitchen. Grace will be back soon from fetching some eggs. We'll get you freshened up, and a good hot cup of tea in your belly. I made some vanity cakes, because I remember how you like them so. I'll reckon you're hungry after all your traveling."

Mama felt her spirits lifting, and she let herself be swept up and embraced by all the smells and sights and sounds.

For the next five weeks, Mama shared the chores of caring for Pa, and helping Ma with the housework. Pa could barely sit up, so they had to help him. She helped Pa turn over when it was time for Ma to give him his bath.

For the first days, Mama never left the house, and she spent most of her time at Pa's bedside. When he was awake, she talked about her life in Missouri, about Rose and Almanzo, about the farm and the orchard, and about the country. She brushed his beard if Ma was busy or tired, and combed his hair. She read to him from the newspapers, or the Bible, until he grew weary and fell asleep.

While he slept, she sat there studying his large, rugged face, darkened from a lifetime of working in the sun. His skin was criss-crossed with wrinkles, each one with its own story, each one a scar from his battle with the land. Pa was an old soldier, she thought, a soldier of the soil.

For Mama, those were the most tender moments she had ever known with Pa. All her life, he had been a great, strong man. When she was little, it only took the sound of Pa's voice to calm her fears. She had seen him stand face-to-face with Indians, and save the whole family from drowning in a creek. He had walked hundreds of miles in battered boots just to harvest another man's wheat to make enough to feed the family.

It was terribly sad to see his strength fading, but Mama was grateful for the chance to give him some small comfort. To hold his hand, to cradle his head while he sipped some broth, to gently wash his face with a damp cloth, was to show her love for him, the way a mother shows her love for her child.

On his good days, she and Ma and Pa and her sisters remembered old stories. They all had a good laugh, even Pa, as much as he could without coughing, remembering the time Mama and Mary played in the haystacks when they lived on Plum Creek in Minnesota, and made all that extra work for him.

And they remembered sadly the little house Pa had built in Indian Territory. That was the house they had to leave, with the garden all hoed and beginning to grow, when the government told Pa he had settled on land belonging to the Indians.

But the best moments were when Mary would sit down at the organ in the parlor and play some of the old songs that Pa used to play and sing for them on his fiddle. Pa couldn't play his fiddle anymore. But they could make music together, and even though Pa couldn't come into the parlor to be with them, he could hear the music and hear his girls singing for him.

On days when Mama felt certain that Pa was feeling a little better, she would let herself go out visiting, or buggy-riding with her sisters. She met Grace's new husband, Nate Dow, and saw their farm some miles outside of town.

She visited with Mr. and Mrs. Boast, who had spent a winter with Mama's family in the surveyors' house, before the little town was built. And she had many visits with her old school friend Mary Power, who lived across the street from Ma and Pa and was married to Mr. Sanford, a banker.

One afternoon Mama went with her sister

Mary to the cemetery to visit the grave of Cap Garland, a school friend Mama had liked. Cap and Almanzo had saved the little town from starving during the Long Winter of 1880. They had driven a sled across miles of snow, in between blizzards, to fetch a load of wheat. Poor Cap had been killed in a threshing accident many years before. Mama left a bouquet of wildflowers on his grave.

She visited the homestead claim where the family had lived when they first came to Dakota Territory, and saw how the cottonwood trees had grown. She visited the claim where she had lived with Almanzo, where Rose was born. It was a great comfort to her to find these places almost as she remembered them, and to share her memories with her old friends and her sisters.

Gradually Pa had fewer and fewer good days. Mama didn't like to leave his side when he was in pain, or deep in sleep. She was afraid not to be there if his time suddenly came.

Then, one day, Pa began to cough and couldn't stop. They sent a neighbor for the doctor. By the time he got there, Pa had fallen into an exhausted, deep sleep. They could not rouse him, and his breath came in shallow rattles.

"It's only a matter of time now," the doctor told Ma. "The best you can do is keep him as comfortable as you can."

Mama barely slept that night, and the next day, and the next night. She sat in Pa's room with Ma and her sisters, taking turns making the meals, and cleaning up. But none of them left the house, except to get wood for the stove, or fetch water, or tend to other necessities.

Pa didn't move the whole time. He just lay there, his chest barely rising and falling. A hot breeze blew in the window, and his lips were parched, so Mama kept them moist with a damp cloth, and gently dabbed his forehead and temples with cool water.

"Laura, dear, why don't you go upstairs and lie down for an hour or so," Ma suggested. "We will call you if there is any change."

"No, Ma," said Mama. "I couldn't. If I can't stay awake at all, I'll just lie down here, on the floor."

Mama did doze off from time to time, but only sitting up, and only for a few minutes. She watched Pa like a hawk, noticing every breath, every slight twitch. She listened carefully to see if his next breath was different from his last. Sometimes she took his hand and held it for a bit, or kissed him on the forehead. And a couple of times she whispered in his ear, "We're here, Pa. Everyone is here with you." She couldn't know if he heard, but she said it just in case.

Early the next morning, she woke suddenly from one of her snatches of sleep. She thought she had heard something, the way a mother hears her baby's cry before the baby has even opened its mouth. She looked at Pa. He seemed the same.

A rooster crowed somewhere nearby. The window was still dark with night. But something was different, and Mama felt her chest tighten.

Then she saw one of Pa's fingers twitching, and she noticed a change in his breathing. The rattle had a new pitch to it, deeper and more troubled.

Ma was sitting in a chair on the other side of the bed, her chin on her chest, snoring. Mary and Carrie had gone to lie down and get some rest. Grace was in the kitchen, putting some water on to boil.

"Ma!" Mama whispered as loud as she dared. "Ma! Wake up!"

Ma's head snapped up. "What is it?" she asked, looking confused and startled.

"Ma, listen. It's Pa's breath. And his fingers are moving. I think he might be waking."

Ma quickly turned up the wick on the oil lamp, and they both leaned over to look into Pa's pale face. His eyelids fluttered a moment, then opened. Mama took one of his hands, and Ma took the other.

"Charles," Ma said simply. "I'm here."

Grace came into the bedroom. One look from Mama sent her running out, to wake Mary and Carrie.

Pa looked weakly at Ma, and then his eyes slowly shifted to look at Mama. She could see the light in Pa slowly fading, and she had to choke back a sob.

Then Pa opened his mouth. "Look, Caroline," his weak voice barely rasped. Mama leaned closer to hear better. He paused a moment, to catch his breath again. "See how Laura's eyes are shining."

Then he closed his eyes again, sighed deeply, and stopped breathing.

For a long moment Mama stared into Pa's face, waiting for him to take another breath. But he lay there absolutely still. A tear splashed on her hand that was holding Pa's. She lifted it to her cheek and said, softly, "Good-bye, Pa. Good-bye."

What Do You Think?

Rose's heart leaped into her throat as the locomotive came sliding into the depot in a gushing cloud of steam and smoke. She searched the windows as it came to a halt with a terrific crash and a last shriek of brakes.

Papa took off his hat to see better, and Rose stood on tiptoe.

The platform swarmed with hurrying people and freight wagons. Papa and Rose scanned the stairs, anxious for their first glimpse of Mama. Finally she appeared in a doorway, and the porter held her hand as she stepped down onto the platform.

Papa strode, almost running, and swooped his arms around her, knocking her hat askew. Rose waited patiently for her turn, then she gave Mama a solid squeeze. It was so good to have her home, after all those weeks.

"Mama, it feels as if you've been away an eternity," Rose said.

"Two eternities," joked Papa. "Tarnation, it's a relief to have you back, Bess. Don't you go running off again, you hear?"

Mama laughed and fixed her hat. "My goodness. Such a welcome! I wonder that I shouldn't go away more often, if this is the thanks I'll get. Let's find my bag, Manly. I just want to get on home and kick off these shoes."

Mama had been gone almost two whole months, the longest two months in Rose's life. She had worked every single day, including Sunday, from before sunup to long after sunset. At first she had been overwhelmed, trying to keep track of all the things that needed doing—the washing, the baking, the cooking, the housekeeping, and then the trips to the farm with Papa to work in the fields or help with mending fences and such.

After a time, she found the rhythm of her days. But there wasn't a night she didn't flop into bed exhausted, often too tired to change out of her chore dress.

She had been the woman of the house, and although she wouldn't ever say she enjoyed it, being Papa's helpmeet was a new experience. She had never felt so grown-up and important, taking care of all the trade at Reynolds' Store, keeping up Mama's account books, and making sure Papa had a good hot meal every day at breakfast and dinner.

She had grown closer to Papa because of it. They had had some wonderful chats at supper, chats between two friends, not just a father and his daughter.

One night Papa had talked some about his childhood, growing up in Malone, New York. Grandpa Wilder, Papa's father, had been a farmer there. He had one of the best farms, with great barns full of healthy livestock and all the hay and oats and corn he needed to feed them.

Then, with all the country looking West, Grandfather decided to sell his farm in New York and move to Minnesota. He built up another good farm. But Papa and his brother, Royal, moved even farther west, to Dakota Territory.

"Why did you leave that farm?" Rose wanted to know as they sat nursing their cups of coffee. "If it was so prosperous, why did you leave?"

Papa chuckled. "There is a question that I have asked myself many times. Royal and I, we thought to start our own lives, with our own farms in the new territory."

He finished filling his pipe and struck a match, pulling the flame into the bowl. He blew out a great cloud of smoke.

"It's a natural thing," he went on. "A young man likes to make his own way, to come out from under his father's hand. The land in

Dakota was free, if we could just hold on to it for five years. There were no trees to fell, no rocks to move. Just open grassland waiting for the plow and the seed. We just knew we would make it big out there."

Rose took a sip of her coffee. She picked up a bit of pie crust from her plate and nibbled. Not as good as Mama's, she thought, but not half bad either.

"Why didn't you?" she asked. "Why didn't the prairie make you prosperous?"

"It's a long story," Papa said wearily. "You've heard all the tales from your mother about what happened. Let's just say that in my life I've had more than my share of disappointments."

Papa's words shocked Rose. She couldn't think what to say for a moment. Then she piped up shyly, "Are you unhappy, Papa?"

"No, no, no!" Papa said quickly, smiling tenderly at her. He patted her hand. "You misunderstand me. I only meant that things didn't turn out quite the way I reckoned. Maybe when I was a young man I was a bit too big for my britches. I expected a lot from life. Father was a prosperous man, and I thought I would be, too.

"The only folks that are never disappointed are them that go through life expecting nothing. And everyone expects something. Everyone has their dreams.

"But all that's behind me now. We have a good life here. And we're a good family. So long as I have your mother and you, there isn't another thing in this world I'd lift a finger to take."

Rose was relieved. It would have been unbearable for her to learn that Papa was unhappy with his life. She had seen him sad. She had seen him angry, although only once or twice. But she had never seen him defeated.

Even so, she thought about what she expected from her life, and wondered what she might say one day to her own son or daughter about it.

Rose had a big disappointment of her own while Mama was away. Professor Lynch wrote

Mama from Mountain Grove Academy saying all the scholarships for the next year of school were already spoken for.

"I am convinced from your description that your daughter would make a fine addition to our class," he wrote. "Perhaps it can be managed for the 1903 school year for her to attend Mountain Grove. However, I must advise you that our scholarships are limited in number and rather small in size. We hope in time that we may be able to offer more. But for now, our resources are quite limited."

Rose had been so busy with her chores that she barely had time to think about what this meant. Certainly at the very least it meant another year in Professor Bland's class, and another year of her everyday life. It was better not to think of it.

When Mama got home from South Dakota, Rose showed her the letter.

"Oh, well," said Mama. "Perhaps it is for the best after all. We can see how the next year goes. Maybe some way will show itself."

Mama told Rose and Papa all about

Grandpa Ingalls' funeral. The whole town had come out, because the Ingalls family had been the first settlers in De Smet. Grandpa had been a farmer there, a businessman, a carpenter, and Justice of the Peace.

"It was a great comfort to see how people held him in such high regard," Mama told them her first night home over a supper of fried chicken and dumplings that Rose had made specially for the occasion. Rose beamed with pleasure when Mama declared the dumplings perfect.

"As for me, it was terribly hard to say good-bye to him, and then to Ma and my sisters. Who can say when we will meet again? But I have this, at least." She laid her hand on the case of Grandpa's fiddle and stroked the well-worn leather.

All those years before, when Rose and her family left De Smet, Grandpa had told the family that when he was gone, he wanted Mama to have his fiddle. Grandma had given it to Mama before she left to come home to Mansfield.

"You can't know how much it meant to me, to have it by my side on the long trip home," Mama said. "It was almost as if I had brought Pa back here with me. Of all the memories I have of him, the ones that bring me the most joy are the times he played this fiddle, and sang. No matter how dark things might have looked for us, when Pa played the light shone, and we could smile again."

"He was good at it, too," Papa said, draining his glass of milk. Mama pushed her chair back to get up and fetch the pitcher, but Rose stopped her.

"I can do it, Mama," she said. "Let me take care of you tonight."

Mama sat down again, chuckling. "I don't think I've ever been a guest at my own table before."

"Rose was a great comfort while you were away," said Papa. "You would have been proud of her."

Mama stroked the fiddle case again. "It's the first thing I remember, Pa's playing us to sleep when we were little, in the Big Woods of Wisconsin. And by the campfires, all through that awful mud, all the way down to Indian Territory and back across Kansas and Missouri. And then across the whole of Iowa and Minnesota and beyond the Big Sioux clear to Silver Lake, he played the fiddle by the campfire at night.

"We never could—I see it now, though I didn't then—we never could have gotten through it all without Pa's fiddle."

Papa took Mama's hand and looked at her with eyes full of love and caring. Rose wished that moment could go on forever.

"Maybe," Mama said softly, "when my time comes, Pa's fiddle might be played for me."

Rose couldn't bear the thought. She pushed it right out of her mind. So did Papa.

"Well, well," he said gruffly, standing up. "Let me pour you a nice cup of tea, and you ought to try one of Rose's doughnuts she made for breakfast. If I didn't know any better, Bess, I'd swear you made 'em yourself. Now I want to hear all about the folks in town up there. And how did the crops look? I read somewhere it's going to be a bumper harvest for wheat."

For weeks after she got home, Mama told Rose stories about her childhood. She told them while they cooked together, over meals, under the hot sun while she and Rose hoed the corn, while they did out the washing, on any occasion at all. She would just start right up: "I didn't tell you about the time Ma was nearly crippled when a log fell on her leg." "Remember I told you of Mr. Edwards? Well, one Christmas when Pa couldn't get to town to buy gifts for us little girls . . ."

Some of the stories Rose had heard before, and many were new stories Mama wouldn't have told her before because she was too young.

She told Rose, "Do try to remember at least some of what I've said. You may not think much about it now. But a day will come when you will want to know where your people came from, and how we lived. Because no one will ever live that way again."

Although Rose was much more interested in the future than the past, she didn't mind hearing Mama's stories. She had always enjoyed them, and it was a distraction from the everyday chores. But it seemed to her that Mama was in an awful big hurry to tell every story she could remember. She seemed to need to get those stories out of her memory, as if she was worried she might forget them, or forget to tell them.

Soon after Mama returned, Rose's life settled back into its old patterns. The apple harvest that fall was quite good—not as good as the first year, but enough to pay down the mortgage some more.

Blanche went off to Mountain Grove Academy, so Rose saw her only on Sundays after church. Once in a while, every couple of months, a boy would ask to walk her home. She usually said, "No, thank you very much." Once or twice she let a boy she knew from school escort her, with Mama and Papa walking behind, just for the change of it. But no one asked to kiss her, and she would have refused if they had.

As Rose found herself just plodding through her life, putting one foot in front of the other like a mule plowing the same field over and over again, Paul began to fill her thoughts. She had continued to write him, and he continued to answer. She had become bolder with her thoughts.

Feverishly one night she scribbled out in a fit of loneliness, "I miss you so much at times that it is an ache. How I would like to look again into your eyes, and try to guess what you are thinking."

When she reread it, she flushed hotly. She hated mushy letters. But she hurriedly folded the letter, sealed it in an envelope, and rushed down to the post office before she could change her mind and tear it up.

She regretted writing it the minute it was gone. She almost wanted to write another letter, telling Paul to ignore the first one. She waited almost two weeks for Paul's answer. The whole time she was nervous and fretful.

Her heart pounded when Mr. Gaskill finally handed her the envelope with Paul's neat handwriting on it. She ripped it open right there and read hungrily.

"Thank you for your last letter," Paul wrote. "I enjoyed it the most of all your letters. I do not think you would ever have need to guess what I am thinking. You know me too well."

Rose's heart leaped for joy. She carried the letter around in her apron and reread those sentences a dozen times in the next few days, trying to divine their full meaning. Was Paul saying he liked her, in a special way? Did he mean that he and she had the same thoughts? Doubts buzzed about her like pesky horseflies. Did Paul mean only that he and Rose had grown up together, like brother and sister? Oh, it was so hard to know, without looking into his face!

Finally, at Christmas, Paul came home for a long visit, two whole weeks. Rose was there with Mrs. Cooley and George to greet him. She had been up late the night before, fussing over her dress, and trying a new way to do her hair.

Once again her heart fluttered in her breast. When he finally came down the steps, she nearly sobbed with joy. He just kept getting more manly and handsome. Paul kissed his mother, shook hands with George, and then looked at Rose. A strange puzzled look came into his eyes, and his mouth made a crooked, shy grin.

He didn't hug Rose or kiss her. He shook her hand. But in his eyes Rose saw a new awkwardness that she had seen many times in the eyes of the boys and young men who waited outside of church every Sunday. She blushed hard.

"Hello, Paul," Rose said.

"Hello, Rose," he answered. "Gosh, it's good to be home."

As it had been the last time Paul came home to visit, Rose barely had a chance to be alone with him. She enjoyed his company, and she caught him looking at her now and then with that strange look in his eyes. But because they were with their families, their conversations were stilted and proper.

On Christmas Eve, Paul went with his family and Rose's to church to help with the decorations. Mama gave Rose a bundle of sprigs of bittersweet and said, "I think this would look nice around the door to Reverend Mays' office, next to the Sunday school room. Why don't you two take that hammer over there and some tacks and see what you can make of it?"

The Sunday school room was in the small wing of the church, away from the main chapel, where everyone else was busy putting up greens and decorating the tree. Rose set the bundle down on the floor by the door, picked up a sprig, and held it against the door molding.

"What do you think?" she asked Paul.

Paul set the hammer down on a chair and came close to Rose. He looked into her eyes and said, "I think I wonder if you can guess what I'm thinking right now."

"Don't be foolish." Rose giggled. "Of course I can't."

Paul took Rose's hand. "Come and sit here. I want to talk."

Rose's stomach flip-flopped. She followed him and sat down on one of the little Sunday school chairs. Paul sat next to her.

"What are you going to do with your life, Rose?"

Rose made a face, part surprise and part confusion. "I don't know," she finally said. "I told you, I was thinking to go to Mountain Grove Academy, but Mama said . . ."

Paul startled her by leaning forward and putting an arm on the back of Rose's chair. Its being there was like a secret shared between them, to be cherished and to be kept unspoken.

"Remember all that time before, when I showed you how I was learning telegraphy, and you said, 'I could do it'?"

"Yes," Rose said quietly. Paul was looking at her with his dark eyebrows knitted together, and his dark eyes gazing deep into her. She didn't mind so much, but still she felt something tighten in her chest, the way it did when she was younger and about to be scolded.

"Well, why couldn't you? Why couldn't you learn telegraphy? If you did, well . . . it might be fun if you were actually an operator, Rose. Lots of girls are having careers these days. Why, who can say, we might be in the same town!"

He laughed roughly and sat back, taking his arm from Rose's chair back. "Why, I could help you with the train orders, and if I worked nights you could fix dinner for me."

Rose's head began to spin. Slowly it dawned in her mind that Paul was saying something important; something just about them, and no one else.

Rose stared into her lap. Her heart was racing, and no words could form themselves in her mouth. She had never felt closer to him than she did in that moment, and it scared her.

"Well," Paul finally said. "What do you think about that?"

"I think it would be lovely, Paul," she said earnestly.

Paul heaved a long sigh. "Gosh, Rose. I get so lonesome sometimes, just me in these towns, and they aren't my towns, or my people. Oh, sure, it's good clean work, and fifty dollars a month. But I miss talking to you, and a fellow can't help thinking, you know. Just thinking, well, what if? I mean, you and me, we've got so much in common, and I'm not getting any younger. Did you ever wonder about that?"

"Yes," Rose said. "I have wondered about it a lot. I have wondered if we, I mean, if you . . . if you felt the same things I do, about life and the future and . . . and us," she managed to say before she could stop herself.

"Me too," Paul said eagerly. "Me too. Imagine that! It's funny, the way we've known each other just about forever and I never thought much about it. But, well, seeing you at the depot, and now. Gosh Rose, you're just the best, the smartest, the sweetest girl in the world!"

348

Suddenly Paul's hands were on Rose's shoulders and he was drawing her closer to him. She felt an urging, like a strong current, sweeping her away toward something unknown, vast and beautifully terrible.

Then a wave of panic seized her. She pushed him away and heard herself saying, "No, no! Please . . ."

He pulled his hands back and slumped in his chair. Now Paul was blushing hard. "All right—if you don't want—I didn't mean—" he stammered.

Then he looked at her with suddenly stricken eyes. "Is it another fellow, Rose? I mean, are you courting with someone?"

"No. No!" Rose protested. "No, nothing like that. I couldn't think of it. I mean, not if you . . ."

Paul took her hands in his. "Look, Rose. I don't know what to say. There's a chance, I can't be sure. But there's a chance I could be coming back to Mansfield next summer, to take a job in the depot here."

"Oh, Paul, that's wonderful!" Rose cried out.

"I want to be closer to Mother, and I want you—us—to think about the future. If you want to, I mean."

"I want to, Paul," Rose said. She looked into his face, and she felt in every bone in her body that no one could ever be as good as Paul, and that he could make her happy, and she could make him happy. Only she needed to think. Everything seemed suddenly so hopeful, yet so mixed up at the same time.

Just then Mama stuck her head into the room.

"You two better get on with it, or we'll never be done in time for services tonight."

They both jumped up. Paul grabbed the hammer and a tack. Rose picked up the sprig of bittersweet, and they went to work.

They never spoke of their feelings for each other again during Paul's visit, except at the depot as he was about to get on the train. He held her hands and said, "Remember what I said."

Rose promised she would, and then he was gone.

An Unwanted Visit

After Paul left, time seemed to stand still. All of Rose's thoughts were bending now toward summer. Like lilies that had been planted in the shade, she stretched toward the sun. But first there was the winter to get through, and her final months of Professor Bland's high school.

Rose kept herself occupied by reading and by writing letters. She never mentioned their conversation in the Sunday school room to Paul. She kept her letters simple and chatty, filling the lines with small gossip. She had seen his mother, and she was looking well.

His brother, George, had taken a job as clean-up boy at Reynolds' Store. There had been a freight derailment near Seymour that tied up the main line for three days.

She had seen a performance of *Uncle Tom's Cabin*, a play about slavery, at the Opera House. "It was so sad that I could not help but shed a tear or two," she wrote. "And such beautiful thoughts: 'Any mind that is capable of real sorrow is capable of good.' I think that is so true, don't you?"

She didn't mention their conversation, because she wasn't sure what she felt. She wanted as much as ever to go on with her education, to attend Mountain Grove. She thought it was a place where she could make new friends, friends who shared her interest in books and learning.

But she didn't know if she could do that when Paul came home to Mansfield, as he'd hoped. Should she stay in Mansfield, for Paul? She shared her dilemma with Blanche one wintry Sunday afternoon as they sat in Blanche's bedroom.

"You ought to go on with your schooling, Rose," Blanche urged as she packed her telescoping bag to take the evening train back to school. "If you can. Mrs. Lynch tells us girls there's no hurry to get married these days. The whole world is opening up for women, but we have to work harder to get ourselves ahead. If Paul likes you well enough, he will just have to wait."

Rose sighed. It was so hard to know the right thing to do. She wanted to be with Paul. She wanted the joy that she knew they could give each other, being a young couple, maybe even starting a family. She desperately wanted her independence, as well. She wanted her own life and had wanted it for a long time. If she hadn't been poor, she would be packing her bag with Blanche right now, and she wouldn't have to decide about Paul.

"I know you're right," Rose said. "After all, I'm only sixteen. And Mama didn't marry Papa 'til she was practically nineteen."

But still she wavered.

Spring came fitfully. It smiled unexpectedly

on the hills through long days of golden sunshine, coaxing the redbuds and dogwoods to
blossom in the woods, and phlox along the
roadsides. Then it hid itself behind cold
skies, turning its back on the eager petals and
sap-filled twigs, leaving them to the lonely
chill of rain and the bitterness of frost.

Papa, Abe, and Nate took turns trudging
behind the plow. They all felt the coming of
spring in the scented air, and in the soil that had
turned springy underfoot. Looking up at the
sparkling skies, Rose felt a warmth in her veins.

Papa had risen in the early dawn on the
frostiest mornings to ride out to the farm,
before breakfast even, and tramp through the
orchard rows. Rose knew from having seen
him do it before that Papa would bend the
tips of the branches between his anxious fingers and pause to get out his pocketknife and
cut open a few buds on his calloused palm.

He would shake his head worriedly and
look at the sky as if he might read the future
in the cloud patterns.

But to Rose the days were like notes in a

melody. Linnets' song and sunshine stream-
ing through the attic windows, or gray panes
and rain on the roof—they were the same to
her. She woke to either as to a holiday.

Every sight and sound seemed to strike
upon her senses with a new freshness. There
was excitement in the bite of cold water on
her skin when she washed up in the tin basin
on the bench by the door. The smell of coffee
and frying salt pork was extra good. She sang
one of the newest tunes while she spread the
red tablecloth on the kitchen table, and set
out the plates.

> *"You're as welcome as the flowers in May,*
> *And I love you in the same old way."*

Rose had become so caught up in her feelings for Paul that she hardly noticed anyone
else, as if she were alone, wrapped in a joy
they were blind to see, and their dull ears
could not hear. She had reached a certain con-
clusion. No matter which way things went,
she would be happy.

If Paul came home, and he wanted Rose to settle down, she would do that, and she would finally be her own person, separate from Mama and Papa. If she could somehow go to Mountain Grove Academy, she would also be on her own. And maybe Paul wouldn't mind so much for Rose to go to Mountain Grove before she settled down. The way Rose had it figured, no matter what happened, she had something wonderful to look forward to.

Even Mama's tight-lipped worry could not break through her happy thoughts. Mama worked silently one morning, stepping heavily about the kitchen, now and then looking through the window to see if Papa had come back from looking over the orchard.

That morning there had been a film of ice on the water in the rain barrel, and little crystals of frost on the grass when Rose went to the water pump.

Papa finally rode back into the barnyard, tethered the mare, and came clumping up to the back door, stopping to scrape the mud from his boots. Mama flung the door open and said, almost harshly, "Well?"

Papa said nothing, knocking his boot heel against the edge of the step. Then he came slowly in and dipped water from the water pail into the wash basin. The slump of his body in his sweat-stained overalls showed his weariness.

"I guess last night settled it," Papa said dejectedly. "We won't get enough of a crop to pay to pick it. Out of twenty buds I cut on the south slope, only four of 'em weren't black. It'll only be worse on the north slope."

Mama went back to the stove and turned the salt pork, holding her head back from the spatters.

"What will we do about the mortgage?" she wondered.

Rose hushed her singing, but the echoes of it still went on in some secret place within her, safe from this calamity.

"Same as we've always done, I guess," Papa answered at last, lifting his dripping face and reaching for the roller towel. "See if we can get Craig at the bank to renew it."

"Well, he will," Rose piped up. "Surely he will. And, anyway, I'm almost through school and I'll be doing something."

Rose still had no clear idea what that something might be. But she felt a strength and happiness that Mama and Papa in their discouragement couldn't have. They seemed, for the first time, to be old and worn, exhausted by their struggles. Rose wished she could take them up in her arms and carry them to comfort and peace.

But Papa said, simply, "We can't count on anything at this point."

Professor Lynch had written Mama that he would send a letter when he knew exactly whether he could offer Rose a scholarship to the academy. So Rose could do nothing about that until she heard. In any case the spring chores, and graduation with its social events, and working at sewing up her new lawn, took most of her time and thoughts.

One day Papa brought home the mail and sat at the kitchen table opening a letter from his sister, Rose's aunt Eliza Jane, who lived in Louisiana. He read a few lines and then he muttered, "Uh-oh."

Mama looked up from checking the bread in the oven. "What is it, Manly?"

"It's a letter from E.J.," Papa said, still reading. He flipped the page over and read the other side. "She wants to come visit us next month."

Mama closed the oven door and made a face. "Is she set on it, or is this just a speculation?"

"E.J. is dead set about everything," Papa said. "She's even giving the date, the tenth of June."

"For how long?" Mama asked grimly.

"Doesn't say. I reckon it could be a month anyway."

"Oh, bother," Mama complained. "On top of everything else. Oh, bother."

Rose remembered Mama and Papa telling her about Eliza Jane before. Mama had had a bad run-in with her when Mama was a young girl in school in Dakota Territory. She had been Mama's teacher, and Aunt Carrie's, too. Eliza Jane had been mean to Carrie, and Mama had had a terrible argument with her.

Papa said Eliza Jane used to hector him and boss him around when he was a boy, growing up in New York State. "She's a bull in a china shop," Papa had said once.

But Rose had been having a wonderful correspondence with Aunt Eliza Jane. She didn't know if she would like her face-to-face, but in her letters she seemed to be a strong, independent woman. Eliza Jane had been a government girl, working in an office in Washington, D.C. Before that she had had a homestead claim in South Dakota, all by herself. She had traveled and seen some of the world, and she wrote with passion about women's rights and the plight of the common man. Her visit was something Rose could look forward to.

She arrived exactly on the day she

promised, with her little boy, Wilder, who was almost nine years old. It was strange for Rose to address someone by her own last name. Eliza Jane's last name was Thayer. Mr. Thayer had been an older, retired gentleman, who had died a few years before, leaving her a widow. Wilder Thayer was a funny name for a person.

E.J. stepped off the train impeccably dressed, all flounced and lacy, wearing a feather hat. She was as crisp and neat as if she had just stepped out of her front door on her way to church. E.J. was much older than Rose expected from her letters, surely as old as Mrs. Rippee. Her thick hair had been done up in a kind of Gibson girl style, which was the style for all the young ladies. But her hair was mostly gray and her eyes pleasantly heavy-lidded. Her cheeks were plump and pink, her skin was smooth, and her forehead wide and open. She looked around the platform with determination, and when she saw Mama and Papa, she marched quickly toward them.

Little Wilder trailed behind, natty in his brown suit, knickers, boiled collar, and tie. His blond hair was combed flat and smooth on his head. He looked around with uncertainty.

"Hello, Manzo," she sang out, giving Papa a peck on the cheek. "Hello, Laura. It has been too long since we saw each other. And dear Rose."

"Hello, Aunt Eliza Jane," Rose said, dazzled a little. Her aunt was like a one-person parade.

"Oh, don't you even think of calling me that," she said, smiling broadly. "You just call me E.J. Everybody does. And haven't you turned into a lovely young lady. My, my. But Manzo," she said, turning quickly to Papa, her eyes measuring him head to toe. "You are looking far too thin for my taste. I will have to see that you eat better. Heavens, how do you find the strength to work, being all skin and bones?"

Rose caught a grimace on Mama's face, and Papa forced a small smile. "Don't you worry about me," he said. "Laura and Rose take well enough care for my stomach. Now let's see about your baggage."

E.J. filled the whole house, every corner, and every waking minute.

"Now don't you even think of me as company, Laura," she told Mama as she unpacked her bag. She unfolded her apron and hung it on a hook on the back of the door. "I have been an independent woman nearly my whole life, and I believe we ladies must stick together and work together. That is the future of women getting their rights. Sticking together. Besides, I like to keep busy. Idle hands, and all that."

At mealtime she insisted on helping in the kitchen. With three of them working together, there was hardly room to turn around.

"Oh, Laura, why don't you just let Rose go and have some fun with Wilder?" she declared. "After all, the poor darling is probably bored to death."

E.J. insisted on cleaning her own bedroom, and the other spare room where Wilder slept. "I have been a homesteader in Dakota," she said, plucking the broom from Mama's hands. "I may not be a spring chicken anymore, but I can certainly do my share."

Mama should have liked to have an extra set of hands. Rose certainly did. But Mama had her own way, and her own pace, for doing things. Another woman underfoot, and Papa's big, bossy sister to boot, didn't set well. There could only be one woman of the house.

Once Rose found Mama sitting on a saddle in the barn even though the half-kneaded bread dough was waiting on the kitchen table.

Mama looked at Rose guiltily. "I had to get away for a moment, or I was afraid I'd lose my temper," she explained, shaking her head in wonderment. "I declare, if there was a speck of justice in this world, your father would be doing the household chores so I could go out and haul freight or chop wood. After all, she's his sister."

Papa stayed later than usual to his drayage, and spent more time out on the farm, but he couldn't escape. E.J. rented a buggy, all on her own, and went touring, stopping at the farm and tramping across the fields to track Papa down in the corn patch. Papa came home in a silent, grim mood. E.J. came breezing in. "I said to Manzo, Laura, that you folks really ought to think of emigrating to Louisiana. This land here is lovely to look at, but it's so stony, I wonder that you could raise enough corn to keep a mouse alive."

Wilder was a bit wild, not at all like his proper, refined clothing. When Rose took him on a long walk through the countryside, he thought nothing of stealing strawberries out of some farmer's patch, or throwing rocks at the squirrels. She scolded him, but all he did was smirk.

He had been told not to play ball near the porch, because he might break a window. But one day when he and Rose were throwing a ball in the front yard, he aimed and threw it straight at the window. The glass crashed, and while Rose stood trembling, E.J.'s voice called him from inside. He went, whistling carelessly, into the house.

An awful fascination drew Rose slowly after him. She peeped through the door into the parlor. E.J. sat on the tête-à-tête with her little boy gathered on her lap, her cheek against his hair.

"Darling," she said petulantly, "you know how Mother loves you. You're the only little boy I have, and you know how I want you to grow up to be always good and happy. Dearest, you don't know how it grieves me to think that you could disobey."

Rose was about to sneak off when Wilder spied her. He turned against his mother's caressing hand and winked at her. Rose was so shocked, she almost burst out laughing.

In spite of Wilder's devilish behavior, and E.J.'s brassiness, Rose liked them both enormously. She sat enthralled at meals listening as E.J. spoke of her work for Eugene V. Debs, a man who had started a new political party, the Social Democrats.

She said Mr. Debs had the right answer to the problems of the common man. The answer was Socialism. He believed that all working people should join together in unions to fight the owners of the big companies, and the wealthy interests.

"Why, when the working folks in this country would join hands, it would be the greatest force for change in the country," she argued. "It's coming all over the world. The days when the ruling classes can dictate to the rest of us are soon to end."

Mama disagreed. "Every person in America has his free will, E.J.," she insisted. "If a man doesn't like the way he's treated, then he has the freedom to find other work, or move to some other more prosperous part of the country. That's what all of us did, and you did too. And I don't like the violence that seems to follow the Socialists around. All those riots and shootings."

"No revolution was ever accomplished without bloodshed," E.J. shot back. "And as for free will, it would be something if the hiring industries were small and scattered the way they used to be. But everything is an enormous system today. Big industrial empires control the jobs. To have freedom, one must have choices."

No one could win an argument with E.J., and Mama didn't try. Rose didn't know which way she felt on the question, but she did know that E.J. was a remarkable woman, even more remarkable for her age. Yes, she was strident and meddling. Rose knew other women like that in town, but those other women had nothing much to say, except their petty gossip about each other.

E.J. was a thoroughly modern woman, crackling with energy and purpose. She said what was on her mind, and didn't care what folks might think of her for saying it. Rose admired E.J. and wished she herself could be so forceful and determined.

The Future Begins

Not long after E.J. and Wilder came to visit, Rose had two more disappointments. Paul wrote that he would not be coming to Mansfield so soon as he had hoped. He had been offered a very good position in Sacramento, California. The wage was too high to pass it over. If he worked there a year or so, he might save enough to buy a piece of land in Mansfield.

Rose was devastated. She had not realized how much she expected Paul to be back home that summer. No matter what happened, she had come to assume at the least

Paul would be nearby. Rose tried to hide her misery, but Mama knew her too well, and she understood the special feeling that Rose had for Paul. She tried to comfort Rose, but the words sounded hollow and empty.

Then, only a few days after, when Rose came home from a buggy ride with E.J. and Wilder, Mama called her into the bedroom and shut the door.

Mama fished in her apron pocket and pulled out an envelope. "This came today," Mama said, handing it to Rose.

She spotted the return address right away: It was from Professor Lynch. Rose looked at Mama and saw in her eyes a pitying look that told everything she needed to know. Rose's whole body sagged. Her eyes began to sting. She dropped the envelope on the bed, and looked out the window. Wilder was playing with Fido in the barn lot.

"I can't go to Mountain Grove, can I?"

"I fear not," Mama said. "I'm sorry, Rose. If there was some way—"

"No, Mama," Rose interrupted. "Don't think about it. I understand. It's only . . . Oh, never mind."

Rose opened the door and walked into the kitchen. She wanted to go outside somewhere, to be alone and think. E.J. was just putting the tea kettle on the stove. She looked at Rose just as Rose let a small sob escape.

"Why, Rose, whatever is the matter?" Rose just shook her head and grabbed the door handle. But E.J. marched across the kitchen and took her by the arm.

"You just come right over here and sit down and tell your old aunt E.J. what's troubling you."

With anyone else, Rose would have torn herself away. But she had become so fond of E.J. that she didn't mind. She sat down and explained all about Mountain Grove Academy while Mama made the tea. E.J. listened quietly, her hands clasped together on the tabletop.

Rose didn't shed a single tear, although the news was about as shattering as any she might have expected. She didn't tell E.J. about Paul, but when she had finished, she blurted out, "Oh, nothing ever comes out right for me! I don't know why, but it just never does."

"Rose, really," Mama scolded.

E.J. drew herself up and fixed Rose with a fierce gaze across the tablecloth. "Young lady, you are suffering an attack of defeatism. Do you think your mother and father would have survived if they sat around bemoaning life's every little stumble?"

Rose shook her head.

"And look at me," she said with a bitter chuckle. "My grand scheme to have my family close to me in Louisiana. What happened? Father's fortune lost. Then Father died. My poor sister Laura died. My husband died, and then his family descended upon me like a flock of vultures. Do you hear me groan about my terrible life?"

"No," Rose murmured.

"You come from sturdy, independent stock, on both sides," E.J. pressed on. "We have all survived the very worst that life could fling at us. And you shall, too. Now, Laura," E.J. said, turning to Mama.

"Yes?"

"Sit yourself down and listen to me. I have an idea." E.J.'s eyes sparkled with the pleasure of a delicious secret about to be told.

Rose looked at Mama questioningly, but Mama was just as bemused. She sat down at the table next to Rose and folded her hands in her lap, like a good girl on her first day in class.

"There is a new high school starting up in my town, Crowley, Louisiana, this September," E.J. began. She looked at Mama, glancing now and then at Rose. "It so happens I am well acquainted with the principal through my work on behalf of Mr. Debs. Quite a modern educator, a reformist but devoted to the classical studies. I know it will be a fine program, and Rose being such a smart girl, I'm sure she would have no trouble at all graduating in one year."

She paused, waiting for Mama or Rose to pass a comment. But they were too bewildered to speak.

"Well?" she demanded.

"But, I don't understand, E.J.," Mama said. "You already know we cannot pay for Rose to go to any academy, let alone one so far away. And besides—"

"Who said a thing about paying?" E.J. butted in. "You don't think for a moment that I would suggest such a thing? After causing Father to lose his wealth, the least I can do for Manzo is to help educate Rose. I would arrange for her tuition. And as for her room and board, she would live with me, of course, and it would cost you nothing."

Rose's heart began to hammer. She flushed feverishly hot.

Mama's eyes were wide with surprise, and her mouth pinched in thought. But she hadn't said no. Rose shook from a violent wave of excitement.

"But—" Mama began.

"There are no buts," E.J. insisted. "If you had the money, would you send Rose to Mountain Grove this year?"

"Of course," said Mama.

"Well, then, what is the difference? The difference is, the proposition I offer costs you nothing."

"But . . . well . . . E.J.," Mama stammered. "So far away. And Rose our only child, and . . . I don't know. It would be quite difficult." She looked at Rose tenderly, but Rose could see in her eyes the struggle going on in her mind. It was wicked, but Rose couldn't stop herself from plain out begging.

"Mama, please! Oh, please! It would be the most wonderful thing ever. And I do love E.J. so. Mama, if ever I could do anything at all, please, *please* say yes."

Mama looked at Rose for a long moment, then stared into her tea cup. Her shoulders slumped. Rose saw that she had been beaten. Just as quickly as she had begged, Rose wished she could take back her words. She

threw her arms around Mama, and buried her
face in her shoulder. She felt Mama's chore
dress dampen with her tears.

"Oh, Mama," she wailed into the faded calico. "I'm sorry. I didn't mean that I wanted to
go away from you and Papa. It's just that I
want so much to get on with my life. To see
something of the world. I'll come back. I
promise. Just for one year. It isn't so very
long, is it?"

Mama stroked Rose's hair. Then she made
Rose sit up and looked her in the eye.

"I know this is right for you, Rose," she
said. "As hard as it might be for Papa and me
to see you go, I do know it's the right thing."

Mama looked at E.J. and smiled. "You are
very generous, E.J., and it is a great opportu-
nity for Rose to improve herself."

She looked back into Rose's face and
brushed a tear from her cheek. "If you want
this so much, you will have my permission,
and I am sure that Papa will agree with me."

"Oh, Mama. Oh, E.J., thank you so much!"
Rose gushed. "I won't let you down. I

promise. I'll be extra good, and study my lessons and . . ."

Rose went on so that both Mama and E.J. had to shush her. E.J. told Rose she certainly would have to study hard all summer, to make her entrance examinations.

"But you are at least as bright as our brightest students down there," she said. "I'm sure you won't have any difficulty meeting the requirements."

When Papa came home and Mama told him about E.J.'s plan, he leaned against the kitchen sink, speechless, stroking his mustache. E.J. hardly said a word, except to add to what Mama had said. "I feel it is my duty to you, Manzo, to give something of our father to your family. It isn't much, but it would give me the greatest pleasure."

Rose explained, as calmly as she could, that she would be good, she would study hard, and she would be home the next spring.

"Well," Papa finally said, "I reckon it can't hurt anything to try it. But it'll be mighty lonesome around here without you."

Rose gave Papa a great, long hug. Her throat swelled shut, and she couldn't speak. She hated the idea of leaving Mama and Papa alone. It broke her heart. And what would Paul say? It frightened her to think of going to a new place where she knew no one but E.J. and Wilder. How would she fit in? What if she couldn't do the lessons after all?

As Rose tried to make sense of this whirling mass of ideas, she knew, if nothing else, that she had to try. She did not know what she wanted from her life, but her whole being yearned for it. She had been waiting forever for her future to begin. And now, finally, it was.